THE SHERIFF AND THE WIDOW

THE SHERIFF AND THE WIDOW

by

Chap O'Keefe

Dales Large Print Books
Long Preston, North Yorkshire,
BD23 4ND, England.

British Library Cataloguing in Publication Data.

O'Keefe, Chap
The sheriff and the widow.

A catalogue record of this book is
available from the British Library

ISBN 978-1-84262-791-4 pbk

First published in Great Britain in 1994 by Robert Hale Limited

Published in Large Print 2011 by arrangement with
Keith Chapman

Dales Large Print is an imprint of Library Magna Books Ltd.

Printed and bound in Great Britain by
T.J. (International) Ltd., Cornwall, PL28 8RW

1

Lesson for Wolves

'Now there's a purty sight,' murmured Deputy Sheriff Alec Tucker, and raised the sun-yellowed paper blind an extra inch or two in the front window of the Cedar City law office.

Across the room, his boss, Ross Kemp, deposited a steel-nibbed pen in the inkstand on his battered mahogany desktop and stretched his cramped arms. He was a big man in his early thirties with wide shoulders and muscular biceps – a man built for action – and paperwork was not among his loves. He uncoiled his frame smoothly from the swivel chair and joined Tucker at the window, moving on his feet with a lightness uncommon for a man of his bulk.

'The surrey, huh?' he said, tongue in cheek. 'Yeah, it sure is a smart rig.' Every word was true enough. An artist's hand had decorated the shiny black paintwork with ornate scroll-work and gold leaf. Its four, smooth-running wheels were a yellow blur, tinged orange by fine red pinstriping on the spokes. Two matching thoroughbreds, sleek and black, were in the harness. Highly polished brass trimmings glinted in the sunlight.

'Aw, you're joshin' me, Ross,' Tucker said. 'You know I was referrin' to the handsome couple ridin' it ... specially that Mrs Black-wood. Wow! She's one hundred percent, blood-heating woman!'

There was no denying that, either. But Kemp didn't really care to chin about Mrs Jessica Blackwood with his sidekick. A frown creased his bronzed brow. Tucker was right about the Blackwoods being handsome, but it was as individuals not as a couple.

Rancher Boyd Blackwood was in his fifties, under-average in height, but a man of stature with a broad chest and a square-shaped head of dark hair shaded a distinguished grey at the temples. He was also possibly the richest man in the territory, owner of the fine Double-B spread and a shrewd cattleman and businessman.

His wife, shielded by a parasol, was indeed something else. The phrase *femme fatale* came to Kemp's mind. He scarcely knew what it meant, but he'd heard it someplace and despite its foreignness it seemed to fit all the same. Jessica Blackwood was a darkly beautiful woman in her mid twenties, tall, slim and mature – and half her husband's age.

'This little old cattle town ain't never seen the likes of such class,' Tucker pressed on, licking his lips with enthusiasm for the subject.

'That's for a fact,' Kemp grunted. 'Maybe old Boyd should of thought twice before he brung her here. Grown men are apt to act like half-baked kids when she's around, you may have noticed.'

Tucker dragged his ogling eyes back into

the room. Kemp wasn't a sour man, and the deputy thought he knew why the sheriff begrudged his admiration of the rancher's wife.

'Never did understand why she and Miss Ellen never hit it off,' he stated openly. 'Women can take the damnedest attitudes, I guess.'

Kemp's back stiffened and his lips thinned into a straight line.

'Boyd Blackwood's daughter can't be blamed for wanting to steer clear of her stepmother. She can be plumb blatant and provoking where menfolk are concerned. I seen it and Miss Ellen has, too. It'll lead to a mess of problems and Miss Ellen wants no part of it.'

Tucker shrugged. He knew his boss well enough to know when to back off. It was the popular contention that Ross Kemp was sweet on Ellen Blackwood, the rancher's offspring by his long-departed first wife, and had been for these last several of her teen years.

So Tucker lapsed into silence on the matter of the second Mrs Blackwood.

'You know,' he continued presently, and a mite tentatively, 'you know, that young Ellen is gettin' to be a fine prospect for some feller, what with the success she's made of her little shop an' all. A mighty – uh – weddable lady, I reckon...'

'God! I swear you're worse than a match-making old woman, Alec Tucker! You seem to be forgetting Miss Blackwood is a rich man's daughter and a frontier-town badge-packer ain't exactly wise material for a husband.'

'Trouble with you, Ross, is you work too hard,' Tucker opined owlishly. 'That, and you've gotten a too well-honed sense of duty.'

'Drop it, will you!' Kemp retorted.

He gestured toward the far side of the office where a fold-down cot with a neat pile of folded blankets stood against the wall beneath a survey map of the county. This was where he customarily slept.

'I'm already wedded,' he said, blue eyes

flashing. 'To the job. I figure a law officer's only legitimate concerns are to keep his bailiwick peaceable and law-abiding. That's why folks elected me and what I've been sworn in for.'

'Yeah, I suppose that's right,' Tucker said placatingly. 'But I dunno there's many would uphold the same views. Cedar City appreciates it.' He pondered a moment, then finished more boldly, 'Leastways, most of its folks does, though I'm damned if Ellen Blackwood would appreciate bein' passed over on account of public duty.'

Kemp scoffed. 'If she doesn't realise she deserves better, then it's only her youth deceiving her and sometime she'll learn it.'

The sheriff returned his gaze to the glare of Main Street and the gleaming surrey, now pulled up outside the livery barn and receiving the diligent attention of not one but two hostlers.

Boyd Blackwood was already strutting away in the direction of the railyard and the town's commercial sector. This, Kemp surmised, he would quickly traverse till he came to the quieter, part-residential street where he was a regular caller at the home and office of his lawyer, Isaac Siebert. A tradesman carrying a bag of tools touched the brim of his hat to Blackwood as he passed. The act of recognition visibly pleased the rancher. He threw back his square shoulders, the deference balm to his ego.

Jessica Blackwood, with a shopping basket looped over her arm, had mounted the plank sidewalk and was sashaying beneath the awnings, ostensibly inspecting the wares on offer in the town's stores.

She wore a thigh-moulding skirt of fine calico, printed in many colours with a swirling floral pattern, and a black satin blouse cut low across the shoulders in a lace-trimmed style Kemp thought should have been more appropriate to a Mexican peasant. But she affected an air of challenging superiority which allowed her to get away with it. And no one could deny the blouse drew attention to the full swell of her breasts and gave tantalising hints of the concealed ripeness of a perfect body.

As always, she had an audience. Dozing loafers jerked out of their siestas; a boy at Baker's Mercantile found a sudden devotion to the sweeping of a doorway; a hotel clerk positioned and repositioned a vacancy sign in a window. Even the horses at the hitching rails, switching their tails at the flies, seemed to sense the vibrations in the air. They shifted their weight from one side to the other and slewed heads around as though to catch a glimpse of the passing phenomenon.

Kemp scowled on it all from his window. 'Sheep-eyed idiots,' he muttered under his breath. But he noted, too, the pair of respectable matrons who sucked in their cheeks and clucked their disapproval. He couldn't hear them, but could imagine the words they exchanged: 'No good can come out of her, the hussy…'

He didn't think for one moment Jessica was unaware of the vacuous, mooning looks she attracted. Dammit, she was *enjoying* it, relishing the power she had over the fools. She was torturing their glands and their minds with her untouchability, wrapped in the secure but invisible cocoon of her husband's power and influence.

The other thing Kemp noticed about Jessica's passage was that she took good care not to linger in the vicinity of the modest millinery and haberdashery shop run by her stepdaughter. Ironic, he thought, since Ellen's business was one place that could normally be counted on to draw the respectable wives of visiting ranchers.

A pair of roughnecks lurched out through the batwings of the Lucky Horseshoe saloon. Comings and goings in Cedar City were something Kemp made it his business to keep track of. This pair were itinerants, part of a crew of trail herders who'd ridden in yesterday, red, sweating and dusty from driving a four-hundred-head bunch of three-year-old beeves to the cattle pens at the railyard.

The cowpunchers had collected their pay

and, as was the wont of their kind, had done the rounds of the town's pleasure spots ever since, whooping it up in all the ways denied them on a hard, late-summer drive.

To some townsfolk these hombres were riff-raff. They frowned on their animal lusts even as they catered to their wants and helped thin the fat green rolls tucked in the pockets of their weather-faded Levis.

But Kemp recognised that they were part of the town's lifeblood.

He never forgot the place's history. Cedar Crossing had been a small, isolated, dead place – just a dozen log huts – before a land speculator and an entrepreneurial liquor dealer had bought up the district and sold it off in small parcels to hopeful settlers enticed by the promoter's optimism, expressed in the settlement's renaming as Cedar City.

The new owners moved in and a farming community began to develop. Then local businessmen induced a railroad company to extend its line to the town, to realise an ambition to cash in on the lucrative cattle trade. The town boomed after the fashion of others of its like.

In the wake of the free-spending, footloose cowboys came their predators: the hucksters, the gamblers, the ladies of the night (and all other hours), road agents, horse thieves, cattle rustlers...

And dismayed respectable citizens raised an outcry that needed the calming of a strong and diligent lawman. The job had fallen to Ross Kemp, who'd built a reputation for being tough and fair.

Because of the kind of man he was, keeping rowdy cowpokes in line was among the least onerous of his chores. Kemp didn't miss much that went on in Cedar City, though this pair of out-of-town drunks, weaving now along the sidewalk, might have seemed beneath the notice of a busy peace officer.

Kemp's instant wariness, he allowed, had more to do with the fact that in their path stood the bounteously-endowed and daringly-attired Jessica Blackwood. A man with any sort of intuition didn't need a fortune teller to prophesy the set-up augured trouble.

The first hint was an incredulous slackness in the trail drovers' jaws, an added glazing of their eyes. Kemp buckled on his gunbelt and got moving.

'Gawd! She ain't real, pard – she can't be,' the biggest of the two drunks slurred. He tipped back the Stetson on his simian, black-bristled brow and blinked.

His companion, leaner and with a wolfish cast to his eyes, growled crudely. 'Hey, sister, come a li'le closer, will yuh? My *amigo* figgers yuh ain't nothin' but a mirage!' He guffawed and caught at her wrist with a horny hand. 'Jest lemme put a kiss on them luscious lips an' I kin tell Max yuh's all solid flesh!'

Jessica wrenched her arm free and retreated backwards into the space between a rack of women's dresses and the plank wall-cladding of Baker's Mercantile.

'Get your filthy paw off me!' she jerked out in indignant disbelief at the man's effrontery. 'My husband will kill you!'

But her accoster was undeterred. He squeezed after her, trapping her against the store wall and imposing his outspread, groping hands over her prominent breasts, rubbing the slippery black satin over swelling nipples.

She squirmed and sobbed. His big partner Max giggled – a high-pitched, incongruous sound like a schoolgirl would make, till it was cut off by a hiccupping belch. 'Save a handful fer me, Lew!'

'You leave me alone, you – you beast!' Jessica stormed. The deeper breath this forced her to draw was tainted with the rank odour of spirits and sour gastric juices emanating from her tormentors.

That was when Ross Kemp made the scene.

'Lay off, you lousy bums!' he snapped. 'The place for you's the calaboose!'

He grabbed Max by the shirt collar and

big as he was flung him out of his way.

Max tottered unsteadily on his high-heeled riding boots, then reeled against the dress rack. He sat down heavily on the walk, pulling the display on top of him in a suffocating rainbow cascade of cottons and silks.

Lew whirled round in a crouch, hand clawing for the holstered Colt at his right hip. 'Why, you god-damned interferin' bast–'

His cussing ended in a yelp; Kemp's booted toe had sent the shooting iron spinning from his grip out into the street and left his fingers curling uselessly with knuckle-whitening pain.

Max scrabbled free of his fabric bonds. He wasn't so drunk any more. Anger and his spine-jarring fall had evacuated some of the alcohol fumes from his brain.

A gathering audience saw Max go for his gun and gasped a warning to Kemp.

'Behind yuh, Ross!' one man found the presence to cry hastily.

Kemp saw he was too late to stop the

other man's draw. He plunged sideways like a massive oak that had been suddenly felled. And his big right fist closed at the same time on the butt of his own Colt.

He hit the boards with a crash that spectators would afterwards swear rocked the awning supports. A deafening shot from Max's gun fanned over his head and whistled out across the emptiness of the main drag.

He rolled like a mountain cat. His Colt left the smooth leather. A finger tripped the hammer onto a cartridge – and a bullet sped to its mark. At such close range, he could scarcely miss the target. But he hit bullseye, too, the lead smacking deformingly into the iron of Max's weapon.

Disarmed, Max staggered back, agape at the limpness of his broken wrist. He was out of the fight.

But Lew wasn't. He was maddened by drink and frustrated lust. His wolfish face contorted in a snarl of fury, he whipped out a Bowie knife. It was a full, vicious fifteen inches long, the glistening blade sharpened on both sides from the curve to the pointed tip, and it had a handguard of brass to assist its handler to drive home a murderous thrust.

Any lesser man would have been intimidated, but Kemp leaped to his feet, wading in fast and furious.

It all happened in split seconds before the echoes of the gunshots died or the acrid wisps of burnt gunpowder cleared. Kemp seized the barrel of his smoking Colt in his left hand and swung it like a club.

The sharp Bowie knife chipped a deep notch in the gun's walnut butt and burred its edge on the steel frame, but the deadly blade was smashed from Lew's hand. Next instant, Kemp's big right fist slammed into Lew's jaw.

Thunk! The would-be molester's teeth crunched together with an audible snap and his eyes rolled. He fell in a rag-doll heap at Kemp's feet.

'That's larnin' 'em, Ross!' Alec Tucker said, rushing up to lend a hand no longer needed.

'That's larnin' 'em good!'

Jessica looked straight at Kemp across the prone man, a gamut of emotions running through the contours of her even features. Her full red lips quivered with the last traces of fear, her cheeks gained new colour that replaced the whiteness of terror and disgust. Then she became quite still, drawing herself up with a renewed air of her majesty, and her amber eyes sparkled with satisfaction and unquenchable mischief.

She was the centre of Sheriff Ross Kemp's attention. It was an achievement she'd often desired but never accomplished. Why, the man paid more attention to that foal-like daughter of her husband! Ellen let him pay her his chaste affection like some big brother she'd never had; was too silly and inexperienced to whet the virile man's appetite for more.

'I'm truly sorry about this, ma'am,' Kemp said, respectfully dipping his head. 'Do you want to lay a complaint against these galoots?'

'Oh, Mr Kemp, thank you so much!' she gushed breathlessly. 'You were simply magnificent–' She broke off, never getting to answer his question.

A murmur had risen from the onlookers and they broke their circle. Boyd Blackwood, his face congested with fury, shouldered his way through their rubbernecking ranks.

2

Unfair Gunplay

The wealthy rancher took in the tableau with sharp eyes that were clouded with passion.

'The dirty coyotes!' he snarled from between clenched teeth. 'I'm told they had you baled up, my dear ... are you hurt?'

Kemp, like most everyone else, knew that Boyd Blackwood doted on Jessica. Her every wish was his command, and despite her unbridled coquetry and self-exhibition it would have been a brave man who would have dared to run foul of his jealousy. He was a power in the country and could afford the indulgence of his temper.

His wife shook her head and smiled with little-girl weakness.

'Not much, Boyd darling,' she said. 'In point of fact, it was hardly anything at all. Sheriff Kemp got here just in time.' She threw the lawman a brief but different smile, lowering her lids.

Blackwood grunted and tilted his head on his short, thick neck. His jaw jutted grimly and his lips thinned into a grim line.

'I don't take kindly to hoodlums roaming Main Street, Kemp. I shall raise this matter with my friend Judge Ward. What have you got to say about that?'

Kemp bristled. The circuit judge Franklin Ward was political boss of the county and chairman of the Board of Commissioners – in effect, Kemp's overseer.

'There'll be no need to take that tone, Mr Blackwood sir,' he said levelly, keeping his own feelings in check. He thrust his Colt back into its holster and gestured a strong open hand toward Max nursing his busted wrist and Lew groaning his way back to consciousness.

'The fellers were liquored up, and now I

guess they know they're licked likewise! Your wife states she's unharmed. With her leave, I'll give 'em till sundown to get out of town.'

Blackwood sneered at him. 'You will, will you?' His thin lips writhed with barely controlled emotion, but what came next took Kemp totally by surprise.

'I say that ain't enough!'

The rancher whipped a revolver from its concealment under the tails of his superfine broadcloth coat. Without warning, he swung the weapon on Max and fired a heavy, bone-smashing .45 slug into the big puncher's right kneecap.

The violence of the crashing shot, the gasp of the crowd and Max's agonised scream were a single peal of horror succeeded by a moment of awesome silence.

Everyone watched Max crumple backwards and tumble off the sidewalk into the dust. New pain pierced the fog of his fuddled wits. He moaned piteously.

Kemp recovered first. The bullying boss of

the Double-B didn't scare him any when it came to seeing fair play in Cedar City. No one did.

It was the rancher's turn to be surprised. Kemp wrenched the warm revolver out of the older man's grasp with scant regard for his own safety.

'Blast it all, Blackwood! There ain't no call for more shooting. You're taking advantage of disarmed and beaten men, and the law won't allow it. Leastwise, not around here it won't. I'm lifting this firearm till you've cooled off.'

He tucked the confiscated gun in his belt.

Blackwood exploded. 'Why, you insolent whelp! Give that gun straight back here and I'll fill your half-baked legal opinions full of holes!'

An excited buzz ran round the crowd, but Kemp turned his back on Blackwood and pointed to Lew, who was staggering to his feet.

'Alec,' Kemp addressed his deputy, 'help this man get his pardner to the sawbones' surgery, will you?'

Blackwood shook his clenched fist at the sheriff's back. 'This ain't over yet, not by a damned sight!' he blustered. 'No man crosses me and gets away with it. You'll regret this afternoon all your born days.'

Jessica laid a restraining hand on his arm, and her touch seemed to restore a measure of his sanity. 'Leave it, darling. Let's go home,' she cooed. 'You mustn't let the man upset you so. Not in front of a crowd anyhow.'

Blackwood surveyed the engrossed witnesses to his discomfiture, withering them with his furious glare.

'Very well, Jessica,' he then mumbled harshly to her alone. 'But Kemp will pay for this humiliation, I promise!'

He stumped away in the direction of the livery barn, not looking back, confident in the expectation that his glamorous young wife would follow.

She did. But unlike him she spared a long look over her shoulder as she departed.

Her eyes met Kemp's and she shrugged.

His eyes, which she knew were blue and clear, narrowed. But he nodded as though he approved of her success in advocating a retreat.

Jessica gave him her most alluring smile, gratified that he'd observed her intervention to spare him further immediate trouble; daring to think that she might have started to thaw his customary coolness toward her. He was such a red-blooded, physically powerful man, as he'd just so capably demonstrated, that it was a great shame he'd never favoured her with his regard.

She wanted Ross Kemp to be interested in her, to desire her, like other men did. In his case, she might even be prepared to seek out the opportunity to reciprocate intimately. The idea of an illicit relationship thrilled her. Because of her nature, and because she was not a virgin, she recognised that her quickened pulses were another of her body's private but unmistakable signs of response to the aura of vital maleness which emanated from him.

She had her sexual needs – they were at least as strong as her liking for knocked-dead admiration and dumb adulation – and experience told her the means to satisfy those needs were sadly diminished in a husband past middle age. The chemistry between her and Boyd Blackwood was inclined to produce a splutter where she sought the exciting spark of a strong reaction.

So her amber eyes hopefully flashed Kemp her most provocative expression. It was a challenging look that said explicitly, 'Come and take me if you can.'

The sheriff had not been the only person watching with attentive interest the passing parade on the Main Street of Cedar City.

Orson Rymer was a stranger in town. His flashily-suited form was slumped with every appearance of indolence in a canvas chair on the gallery of the Cedar City House hotel. The heels of his highly polished, handmade boots were propped on the gallery railing; a flat-topped sombrero was tilted deceptively over his alert obsidian eyes. Rings glittered on the long, immaculately manicured fingers that drummed easily on the wooden arms of the chair. On the low table at his side, part of a pack of crisp new playing cards was spread in an abandoned game of solitaire, and a cold green bottle, misted by the heat, and a tall glass stood ready to slake his afternoon thirst.

When Jessica Blackwood stepped into his line of vision, hips swinging, Rymer's astonishment was virtually invisible. The casual tap of his supple fingers missed a beat. His hidden eyes widened beneath the hat brim. And that was all.

Jessica!

It had to be her – all woman as ever and typically glorying in it. She'd had no twin he'd heard of, and could a female such as her have so exact a double? Jessica, he'd been one of many to appreciate, was a unique specimen.

A waiter passed, clearing tables. Rymer plucked at his cuff.

'Who is that woman?' he asked in a cool, disinterested drawl, nodding his head in her direction.

The waiter looked across the street, and sucked his breath beneath his teeth with a lopsided, knowing grin.

'Fancy baggage, ain't she, suh? But you'd better keep your eyes off.'

'How's that then?'

'Waal, suh, rumour has it she's no better than she oughta be, but thet thar's Mrs Jessica Blackwood, who's married to the richest rancher hereabouts – an' mebbe the touchiest sonofabitch to boot.'

'Hmm...' said Rymer, settling back again in his chair as though he was giving this deliberate consideration. 'A sassy little piece, I'd say, but I'll keep what you say in mind. Meanwhile, I guess this Blackwood jasper can't stop me looking and thinking.'

'That's right enough. Lord knows, I reck'n she's a witch to draw a man like she does,' the waiter said virtuously and shuffled off on his chores.

Rymer continued his observations. Bar Ross Kemp, he was the first fascinated member of the audience that witnessed Jessica's confrontation with the two drunken trail herders.

His imagination ran riot when Lew crowded her behind the dress rack, but he knew he could see all he needed to from his inconspicuous vantage point on the hotel gallery and he made no move to rescue Jessica from her hassling by the hardcases. He didn't so much as raise an admonitory yell. Actually, a lewd chuckle twitched the too-full lips beneath the thin black line of his rakish mustache. The picturing of Jessica's manhandling sent a trickle of saliva drooling from the corner of his mouth.

Voyeurism gave way to headier entertainment when the sheriff took a masterly hand and six-guns fired and a knife flashed shortly in the sun.

The boorish and needless intervention by the proud and prosperous-looking gent he gathered to be the rancher Blackwood gave

Rymer cause for more serious reflection.

Nor did he miss the subtle hints communicated by the eye contacts made between Jessica and the sheriff: appreciation and invitation on the one part, an edgy reserve on the other. It was part of Rymer's trade at the gaming tables to read body language, and though this case was something else it had its points of similarity.

In particular, Rymer noted Jessica's last look of reluctant parting and patently amorous promise.

'God damn it!' he affirmed to himself. 'She's set her sights on the tinbadge for sure. He's just the macho type she'd pick for a roll in the hay.'

One of Rymer's personal maxims was 'You can't keep a good man down.' Nor, in Jessica's case, he thought, a bad woman either!

It was a delicious situation, coming across her here in such promising circumstances. A stroke of luck, the like of which hadn't come his way in many a moon. He saw the opportunity for immense profit if this Blackwood was as wealthy and jealous as his reputation and recent appearances suggested.

Jessica would have to be apprised of his presence and brought to an appreciation of her dependence on his goodwill. But first he'd need to do some groundwork.

That evening, Rymer smoothly engaged the gossipy night clerk who manned the hotel lobby in lengthy conversation, after which he began to lay plans.

Business was brisk at the Lucky Horseshoe. When Ross Kemp pushed in shoulder to shoulder with Alec Tucker, there was standing room only in the saloon. It was the end of the month and payday for many of the cowhands working the spreads around Cedar City.

An especially rowdy bunch of riders had just arrived in town in a cloud of dust, blazing off guns into the air as they swept along the main drag. The sheriff decided to keep an eye on their progress into their favoured watering-hole. 'That pack of howling hyenas ain't starting trouble in this neck of the woods,' he told Tucker.

Kemp cast an appraising look about the lamplit, smoke-filled room. The whooping crew, once through the batwings, had quietened themselves down somewhat. Its members returned his approving nod with sardonic amusement, knowing from old he would stand no nonsense but that any dealings he might be obliged to have with them would be scrupulously fair.

'Set 'em up, pop!' one waddie cried to the ageing barkeep. 'We're here to have fun!'

The saloonkeeper himself glided his portly bulk along behind the counter to serve the two peace officers personally. 'What'll it be, gents? On the house, of course...'

Kemp and Tucker settled for beers. While Kemp sipped the brew, he took in the earnest business taking place at a poker table in a far corner beyond the general hubbub. He frowned over the frothy head brimming his glass.

Orson Rymer was one of the players. The

dapper visitor was resplendent in a black Prince Albert, a fancy vest with mother-of-pearl buttons, and a string tie. He studied his cards speculatively and inhaled deeply the smoke of a long, thin cheroot.

'You know, Alec,' Kemp confided, 'that man Rymer bothers me some.'

Kemp had kept Rymer under his discreet surveillance since soon after he'd arrived in Cedar City. Like always, he'd made it his business to check up on a stranger in town.

'Why should a professional gambler want to hang around a small town like this for a month or more?' he went on. 'Don't seem natural.'

'Dunno, boss, but he's a wizard with the pasteboards. He's purely rakin' in the *dinero* over there.' Tucker threw a meaningful look out of the corner of his eye at the pile of coin and bills stacking up in front of Rymer.

Kemp shook his head. 'It doesn't figure... And another thing was how he left town for several days a couple of weeks back but didn't give up his hotel room.'

'He had business someplace else…? I hear he drifted down from Colorado.'

'Come to think of it, that probably is where he snuck off to. But what kind of business would he have to go to? And what was bringing him back? He ain't the kind that lives by honest labour. He's the lone wolf living on his wits and unscrupulous ways. I seen 'em before, Alec. A smooth way with ladies and businessfolk – not to forget a quick hand with the cards and eventually a gun!'

Deputy Tucker gave an uneasy sigh.

'The man's done nothin' we kin hold agi'nst him yet, Ross. As it stands, we'll jest have to watch and wait.'

3

Ellen

Orson Rymer permitted himself a brief smile of satisfaction and let the cheroot smoke trickle from his flared nostrils. Kemp's troubled vigilance sharpened.

The lawmen's beer glasses had been drained and in that interval a build-up of tension from the corner poker table had spread tentacles through the saloon. The noise level fell back to a hum of avid interest. Kemp could now hear the murmur of voices, the chink of coin and the soft flipping of the cards on the felt as the hands were dealt.

The stakes were climbing mighty high. Kemp marked a certain, strained nerviness about the thin-shouldered man who had his back to the room, across the green-topped table from the flashily dressed gambler. The way he sat was eloquent. He was losing heavily and couldn't afford to.

Kemp turned to the counter and switched his eyes to the same scene reflected in the ceiling-high backbar mirror. 'Jeremiah McClay, ain't it?' he quietly asked his deputy.

Tucker nodded. 'The Snake hisself,' he confirmed. 'But he's outa his class this time. If he turns his head ag'in, yuh'll see his ugly face gawn as pale as a fish's belly.'

McClay exulted in the nickname Snake because he believed it a tribute to his striking swiftness in the drawing of a handgun and the shuffling of a pack of cards. He saw himself as a swell sport and a real sharp bucko. In truth, he was a fiddle-foot cowhand currently enlisted, to Kemp's disgust, on the Double-B payroll.

'The bum must've gone beyond his limit. He's writing IOUs to stay in the game,' Kemp informed Tucker, keeping tabs in the mirror.

One of the other three players suddenly pushed back his chair after betting heavily and losing. 'That's my lot, gents. Yuh won't mind my pullin' out after I've fattened the pot, will yuh?'

'Count me out, too,' the man on his right said with a philosophic shrug.

Rymer's dark eyes caught and held McClay's shifty gaze. 'I reckon the game's over, Mr McClay.' He took up one of the cowpoke's pencil-scrawled notes in his beringed fingers and waved it delicately. 'I think you'd have trouble raising enough to call me. There's already a little matter of two hundred thirty-some dollars outstanding...'

Tucker nudged Kemp. 'Thet's more'n five months o' McClay's pay!' he whispered.

'Yeah,' McClay growled truculently. 'Yuh offered to accept notes I writ, didn't yuh? I never know'd a run ag'inst me like it. It damnwell beats the law of averages. I was suckered!'

A cynical smile played around Rymer's

fleshy lips. 'The luck of the cards, Mr McClay. But there's no call for harsh words between friends and gentlemen. I suggest we discuss the business *privately.* Could you do me the favour of stepping across to my room at the Cedar City House?'

Both men left soon after, separately, Rymer delaying his departure to toss down a double measure of bourbon at the bar.

Snake McClay went with a swagger. He wasn't a man to crawl, ever, though this evening's experience had been a galling one, Kemp divined.

A stringy, monkey-faced little runt probably in his late twenties, McClay was a hard-bitten, vindictive sort of man, proud and stubborn. He had cold grey eyes, customarily blank as though masking secret thoughts. Prematurely balding, a fringe of lank hair surrounded a patch of flaky-skinned scalp while he hadn't shaved in several days and stubble sprouted on his chin, giving it a dirty look.

At the batwings he paused to give his

Double-B pards a surly wave. 'See yuh later, boys!'

'He ain't exactly tuckin' his tail an' runnin',' Tucker commented, his tone full of contempt.

Kemp concurred gruffly. He had the sneaking suspicion that a trap had been set and sprung. But who was the victim?

McClay had no money, nor any prospect of it. It looked very much like the gambler was going to have to accept that the cowpoke's debt to him could only be written off. At a guess, they would come to an 'arrangement' behind closed doors that would jeopardise the reputation of neither.

But Kemp had his misgivings. He told himself to quit being fanciful, yet went on trying to make it add up more satisfactorily in the light of them.

Next morning, acting on an impulse, he sent off an enquiry by wire to the state capital.

Ellen Blackwood paused under the simple

sign that said 'Ellen' above the door of a modest millinery and haberdashery shop just off Main Street and fumbled in her purse for the key.

She wasn't by nature a fumbling person. A quality of inherent repose usually lent a grace to her every movement. But this moment she was angry. She'd just returned to her home, which was at the back of the shop, from a visit to her father's big rock-and-adobe ranch house on the Double-B.

She wore a pearl-grey sombrero, yellow bandana, a light flannel shirt – it might have been called mannish except the snug fit did nothing to disguise delectable curves – and a divided corduroy riding skirt.

Fiercely independent though only nineteen, Ellen abhorred anything that might be construed as meddling in her private affairs. And it was this that had put her out of countenance.

Bringing the key finally to light, the girl thrust it into the lock and let herself in. A bell above tinkled briefly before she closed the door and swept across the shop and behind the heavy tapestry drapes that partitioned off her living quarters.

Here she flung off the sombrero, loosing the pendant ringlets of her golden hair, so that they bounced lustrously in the morning sunlight shafting through a rear window. She also quickly removed the shirt and skirt, dusty from the trail. Tipping water from a pitcher into the fine blue chinaware bowl on the washstand, she quickly sluiced face, neck, hands and arms to freshen up before putting on a cool gingham dress that, though she wasn't conscious of it, complemented the unbroken bloom of her youth.

All the while her head was filled with images of Sheriff Ross Kemp. She'd go to hell before she'd do what her father had told her!

When she returned to open up the shop, fate had it that the first person she should see passing by was Kemp. Without hesitation, she flung open the door. A glad cry of surprise burst from her lips.

'Mr Kemp! Oh, Mr Kemp,' she called, 'I have to speak to you!'

Raising his hat, and his eyebrows, too, Kemp broke his measured stroll. 'Why, Miss Ellen, what is it? You look in a fair lather about something...'

Ellen's flushed cheeks took on a still deeper hue as he came over and followed her into the little shop. His powerful frame seemed to fill all the available space between shelves packed with hatboxes, the colourful bolts of cloth and spools of yarn and thread.

'Come and sit yourself down a moment, if you please, Mr Kemp. There's something I wish to tell you.'

Kemp was intrigued and slightly perturbed. Ellen was not a girl to get in a fuss about nothing. He weaved an agile path between two glass-fronted showcases containing needles, buttons, ribbons and other feminine necessities to where a small cedarwood table and two chairs completed the furnishings.

'It's about my father, Mr Kemp. I rode out

to the home lot today to visit him.'

The sheriff placed his hat on the table and pulled out a chair for his host. 'He was well, I trust.'

Kemp knew that after Ellen's refusal to carry on living under the same roof as her glamorous stepmother Jessica, Boyd Blackwood had reluctantly agreed to let his daughter come to town and had provided the capital to set up her business.

Ellen was a competent young woman. The shop had prospered, its young operator displaying all her father's business flair coupled with an appealing freshness and warmth. But though Kemp believed Ellen had hidden reserves of quiet fortitude, he realised there must be times she regretted the abrupt and untimely uprooting from her childhood environment.

Boyd Blackwood seemed insensitive to the oddity of the situation. He doted on his young second wife to the extent that it left blind spots in his judgement. Luckily, in this instance, the result was turning out well enough. Or so it had seemed.

'Yes, my father was in his usual robust health,' Ellen said, though with an absence of pleasure. 'But I happened to – er – mention your name, and he flew into the most fearful rage.'

Kemp frowned. 'I guess he hasn't gotten over my taking his revolver off him. That was a month back and he hasn't reclaimed it yet. Too proud, maybe.'

Ellen shook her head nervously and dropped her eyes, as though ashamed to speak out further.

'No, it's more than that, I fear. He said he has evidence to break you, and he vowed to do just that! He was so passionate about it ... like he is usually only when something has happened involving Jessica.'

Kemp patted Ellen's slim hand, thinking absently how smooth the skin was, like the texture of rose petals.

'We mustn't let it worry us. I don't hold your father's follies against you. We can still be good friends.'

Ellen's soft hazel eyes flew wide and shining. 'Oh, but we can't!' she cried. 'He insists that after I've advised you of his intentions I'm to have nothing more to do with you!'

She didn't dare to say that she would willingly defy this edict.

Kemp was stunned by the ultimatum. 'That sounds crazy, Miss Ellen. He can't intimidate a law officer. Wasn't he any more explicit about what's bugging him?'

Ellen shook her golden curls. 'No, he was ridiculously secretive. That is, he said it was nothing fit to be heard by young ears, but you would understand and could expect to hear from him very soon.'

Kemp tried to make light of the mystery. 'Aw, well, your pa has done some strange things before,' he said with a laugh. 'Like taking on that pasty-faced saddle-bum Jeremiah McClay. That I never did understand.'

'Ugh! Snake McClay! Why do you mention the odious man?'

Kemp told her briefly how the Double-B cow-waddie had ostensibly signed away the equivalent of several months' earnings to the man called Orson Rymer, who was clearly a professional gambler and seemed to have taken up residence at the Cedar City House.

'McClay turned up in the weeks after dad returned from Colorado with Jessica,' Ellen remembered, slightly wrinkling her smooth brow. 'It was after the fall roundup. He said he was riding the grub line.'

Kemp understood that she meant McClay was resorting to the time-honoured cowboy custom of riding from ranch to ranch, taking advantage of typical rancher hospitality, fulfilling any odd jobs that cropped up, like fence building.

'He was a real mean customer,' the girl continued, 'and I hated the way he used to leer at me and follow me with those cold eyes of his when he thought I didn't know he was around. If he ever had a message to bring, or a chore to do around the house, he'd try to find an excuse to touch me, too. It was horrible. He gave me the shudders, and I think he knew I despised him.'

The sheriff's big hands clenched involuntarily into fists. A brooding light came into his blue eyes.

'How did he make out with the rest of the crew?' he asked, his tone gruff.

'Not very well, I think. He'd spend most of his spare time in the yard behind the bunkhouse, practicing his draw, shooting at old cans for targets. It was the thing he was best at and most proud of. He got the boys to call him "Snake", but I was amazed when father took him on full-time. Looking back to those early days of his marriage to Jessica, I think his judgement was impaired; he was besotted with the new bride.'

Kemp wasn't reassured by Ellen's summing-up of the unattractive little amateur gunman.

'Well, now McClay is in debt to this Rymer dude, and when no-goods need *dinero* bad, it starts to worry me what they might get up to,' he mused.

After a moment's frowning reflection,

Ellen licked her shell-pink lips. She said quickly, 'I don't know that I should mention it, because it's probably of no importance, but by an uncommon coincidence I saw today this other man you mention – this Orson Rymer…'

'Oh?' Kemp prompted gravely, sensing more was to follow.

'I rode back from the Double-B through the hills, past the old Holyoak place. And behind the ruins of the homestead I saw the strangest – er – meeting.' A blush crept to the roots of her hair. 'I didn't mean to pry and I pulled back into the brush before they saw me, but I recognised the people instantly. How could I not? One was my stepmother, Mr Kemp, and the other was Orson Rymer.'

A low chuckle escaped Kemp's lips.

'I guess it's no secret to anybody Jessica draws all kinds of admirers,' he drawled quietly. 'Leastways, to anybody but Boyd Blackwood. Jessica must be a loco fool if she thinks she can cheat on your father, but that isn't *our* problem.'

Ellen took an oddly delicious comfort from the way he emphasised the word 'our'. Did it mean this strong, thoughtful man was prepared to share her other concerns?

Kemp was not as shocked as Ellen to learn that Jessica had kept an apparent tryst with the smooth tinhorn. The man had a suave charm and the even-featured looks women night construe as handsome. Yes, Rymer was a lady's man all right, and the type who wouldn't hesitate to take his pleasure from any chances arising.

Kemp saw no more to it than that.

And if there was a secret liaison, it could explain Rymer's continued dalliance in town, though Kemp somehow couldn't see the gambler letting his heart rule his head. He could better imagine him being prepared and able to pay for his fun in the parlour-houses of Virginia City, Nevada, or Leadville, Colorado.

Kemp took his leave. '*Adios,* Miss Ellen. Don't worry about your father now. His bark is surely worse than his bite.'

Ellen gulped, unable to confess that amidst the unpleasantness she was more worried for him than her father. But she managed to shape her sensitive mouth into a smile.

'Look after yourself, Mr Kemp, won't you?'

The talk of Snake McClay had reminded Ross Kemp of the enquiry he'd sent over the wire to the capital. He strolled down to the telegraph office at the railroad depot.

The shirtsleeved operator was busy tapping out a message on the key of his apparatus, his finger swiftly and nimbly translating the words into morse code.

'Be right with you, Sheriff,' he called pleasantly. 'Got a message for you not an hour ago.'

Finishing, the man turned to a row of pigeonholes on the wall of his cramped office and brought over to the window a message form filled out with neat block capitals.

Kemp read, and a gleam of satisfaction brightened his eyes. The territorial officials had done him proud, running down the facts on Jeremiah McClay.

'Well, my hunch was right,' he muttered to himself. 'Our friend Snake was previously a jailbird. I always did think he turned up here with a prison pallor!'

McClay had been convicted for stage robbery and attempted murder and had served a seven-year sentence.

It was also noted McClay had been suspected of rape, but his shocked victim had been too deeply mortified to testify.

4

Rancher's Rampage

Dusk had settled over Cedar City and was deepening into night. A crisp breeze skipped playfully down Main Street, funnelled by the false fronts of the wooden buildings. It swept the dust under the boardwalks in eddies and worried a flapping news-sheet into erratic flight.

Cooling timbers creaked and crickets chirped in a continuous chorus that would have been remarked only if it had been suddenly to end. Somewhere in the empty hills, way beyond the boundaries of settlement, a coyote howled mournfully at the rising moon.

It had all the makings of a quiet, midweek night in town.

Late afternoon, Boyd Blackwood had ridden in alone on a steeldust roan with white markings that dramatically set it apart from most other mounts tethered at the hitching rails.

The rancher was in a black mood. His first call had been made on lawyer Isaac Siebert, where he deposited a document. It was on a roll of thick, parchment-like paper and was tied with red tape. He'd then stumped back into town.

A hostler, lounging on a bale of hay at the yawning entrance to the livery barn, noted he was untypically indecisive in his movements, like a man shattered by bad news – a death in the family perhaps. But the prosperous rancher wasn't a man approachable by his inferiors, which is how he would have regarded most of the town's working people.

His face set in hard planes, Blackwood ultimately directed his heavy footsteps to the sheriff's office.

Alec Tucker put down a dime novel and scrambled to his feet when Blackwood thrust open the door.

'Mr Blackwood! Is there somethin' I kin do fer yuh, sir?'

Blackwood's flinty eyes flicked round the office.

'No, there ain't, Mr Deputy! Where's Ross Kemp?'

'He went outa town fer the county clerk. Some small argument arisin' over the regis-terin' of a brand. If'n it's about your gun, mebbe I kin help.'

'Blast the gun! I want Kemp! Tell him I'll be back!'

Blackwood had stormed out and later enquiries established he'd started at one end of town and worked his way to the other, stopping at every saloon on the way. By nightfall, he was well liquored up.

Barkeeps reported he wasn't good for business, apart from the drinks he morosely ordered for himself. He was rude and peremptory and glowered at other patrons. Attempts at polite conversation with him were cut dead. He just nursed his drinks and stared into empty space.

Around about nine, Blackwood lurched out through the batwings of the Lucky Horseshoe. For a moment, he stood swaying in the pool of light that spilled out onto the porch.

'K-Kemp!' he grated.

Then, getting his bearings, he stumbled away into the darkness, his boots clumping echoingly on the planks of the sidewalk.

Ross Kemp had long since returned to town and was settled behind his desk completing paperwork preparatory to turning in for what he confidently expected to be an early night. The blankets were already unfolded on the cot at the back of his office.

A fist pounded on the frosted-glass pane in the door and the doorknob rattled.

'Open up, Sheriff! Open up!' The voice was slurred, unrecognisable.

The caller hammered again and Ross feared the tough glass might break. 'All right, I'm coming! Hang on, will you?'

The sheriff's relaxed muscles jerked into action and his big frame uncoiled like a tense spring, taking him across to the door where he shot back the bolts and freed the latch.

The door was instantly shoved into his face.

'Say, what is–'

Blackwood burst into the office.

'So y' here *this* time,' he sneered. 'Been out chasing more skirt all afternoon, I guess!'

'Blackwood! What kind of crack is that, might I ask?'

The rancher took several tottering steps across the room and leaned heavily on the desk.

'Huh!' he snorted. 'Don't come the innocent with me – you dirty, wife-thieving bastard!'

Kemp shook his head as though he wasn't hearing properly. Alec Tucker had warned him Blackwood was on the warpath, but he'd had no idea why.

'Now let's get this aright,' he said incredulously. 'Are you accusing me of taking liberties with some man's wife?'

Blackwood jigged with rage. 'With *my* wife, damn your eyes!' he roared.

'I don't know what you're talking about, Mr Blackwood.' Ross smelt the sweet-sour odour of alcohol emanating from his irate visitor. 'I suggest you've been drinking overmuch and the liquor has run away with your tongue.'

'You insolent skunk!' Blackwood rasped venomously. 'Ain't no use denying it. I seen the secret notes you've been slipping Jessica. All the more, I know you've been acting like you were sweet on that filly of mine, Ellen. That was just a blind. Real devious business – and heartlessly misleading a young, inexperienced gal! But I'm gonna expose you to Judge Ward. You'll be disgraced and slung out of office!'

'This is rot. I've writ no notes...' Kemp said wonderingly.

'You have so! And you were a goddamned fool initialling 'em. So now I've got you where I want you, Mr Bossy Sheriff!'

The hurled, liquor-thickened retort preceded a bull-like rush.

Kemp sidestepped and Blackwood's careering fist grazed past his ear.

With a cry of drunken wrath, the thick-set cattleman went staggering on till he was brought up by a chair which thudded back into the adobe rear wall releasing a trickling shower of dusty particles.

Blackwood was enraged still further. Stooping, he picked up the chair in one hand and swung it murderously at Kemp's head.

Kemp ducked. The chair toppled a hat-stand, both pieces of furniture smashing splinteringly to the floor.

With another bellow, Blackwood came lunging forward again, fists like hams flailing.

Kemp copped a ringing blow to the side of the head. 'Cut it out, Blackwood – or you'll pay dearly!' he rapped.

But the rancher had worked himself up till

he was insensible to warning. He took another swing at Kemp's jaw.

'You've asked for it, Blackwood,' Kemp grunted, bunching his own big fists. He stepped in under the other man's right arm and lammed his punch wrist-deep into his drink-bloated belly.

An almighty belch ripped from Blackwood's snarling lips and he doubled up.

Kemp was almost overcome by the sickly gush of breath, but he followed through. His left shot in a rapid arc to Blackwood's jaw, rocking him back on wobbly legs.

But Blackwood was made of strong stuff. He recovered to croak an obscenity. 'No man does that to me!' Then with unexpected swiftness, he shot out a booted foot.

Crunk! One hardened square toecap of a pair of thirty-dollar Justins struck Kemp paralysingly on his unguarded shinbone. He lost his balance, falling against the desk.

Blackwood immediately closed in, to follow up his new advantage. He landed a heavy blow, splitting the skin over the bone above Kemp's left eye socket. Blood welled and trickled, spattering the sheriff's star-adorned vest.

Kemp weaved, dodging Blackwood's merciless but unscientific onslaught. He pivoted on the heel of his good foot and the next punch he delivered was a telling one.

A mist of blood blurred his vision and his smashing fist caught Blackwood's plunging form on the nape of the neck.

It was a rabbit-punch which, if delivered with more force, might well have lethally snapped the top of Blackwood's spine.

As it was, it put him face-first on the floorboards, barely conscious, like a pole-axed steer, his stocky arms now limp and outflung.

The office was all at once still and silent, except for the sound of Kemp's own ragged breathing. He was panting from exertion and a hundred bruising pains.

He yanked open a drawer and reached in unsteadily for a pair of handcuffs. Checking that the key was on the ring at his belt, he pulled Blackwood's wrists together and manacled them. Then he rolled the battered man onto his back and propped him up against the desk.

Kemp slumped into his big swivel chair and mopped at the blood still oozing from the cut over his eye.

'Drunk! He must've been drunk,' he murmured. 'But what was all that stuff about me writing notes to Jessica? I don't get it…'

Fooling around with the teasing dark temptress would make about as much sense as playing with a stick of unstable kieselguhr dynamite.

It suddenly struck Kemp with almost physical force that this whole sorry set-up was going to embarrass and upset Ellen Blackwood. His blood boiled at the thought. For some reason, he felt that was something he had to move heaven and earth if necessary to prevent. Judging by the state of him, old man Blackwood had been drinking up large all over town. Which would have gotten tongues wagging aplenty, even if he hadn't already blurted out his crazy accusations in the Cedar City saloons.

'What a mess,' he groaned. 'Mebbe Blackwood will make more sense when he's recovered from his drinking jag. Hell, I can't figure it out at all. But I don't fancy another round with the hombre.'

Kemp pulled out his Durham sack and pondered his options while he built a smoke. It wasn't easy wearing the badge they voted you to have, and Blackwood was a bad man to buck. But a man had to live with something a lot more important than the good opinion of influential electors. He had to live with his conscience.

He scraped a lucifer on the edge of his desk end and, as he put flame to the twirl of wheatstraw paper and tobacco flakes, decided the best way to avoid a developing scene was to lug the rancher into a cell, where he could sleep it off. The jailhouse was right behind his office in a separate but adjoining structure.

After a few puffs of his cigarette through

punch-swollen lips, Kemp hauled the moaning rancher up and dragged him on his heels to the solidly panelled door that was one entrance to the lockup.

The sheriff unlocked the door and pulled Blackwood through.

'Welcome to the calaboose, Mr Blackwood. We don't often entertain the likes of rich ranch owners, but it's clean, tidy and quiet – and just the place to cool off.'

The walls were thick adobe on all sides and the floor was stamped dirt. The cells, three in a row, each had a heavy iron-grille door that went from ceiling to floor, and a stack of old, much-washed army blankets on a wooden bunk.

'No one'll hear your moaning in here,' Kemp informed his prisoner matter-of-factly. 'Nor the raving if you should take it into your head to start that up again!'

Knowledge of his whereabouts percolated to Blackwood's brain. His slitted eyes glimmered in the half-light.

'This time Franklin Ward *will* have my

report, Kemp,' he slurred. 'I'll see you broken – and no way can Jessica persuade me otherwise now I know your game.'

When Boyd Blackwood had headed into town that afternoon, a second horseman had followed surreptitiously in his tracks, without compunction neglecting his lone duty on an outlying Double-B pasture to do so.

Snake McClay these days had a second master to please.

The monkey-faced gunnie scratched his balding scalp when the rancher visited lawyer Siebert's and was even more puzzled by his antisocial behaviour in various barrooms along the main drag.

His boss seemed to be trying to tune in to the town gossip, as though expecting to hear something of importance – which in Blackwood's case meant something concerning himself or his sexy young wife – but his arrogance was as entrenched as ever and he conversely shunned all intercourse.

It wasn't hard for the stringy little Double-

B rider to escape notice. Blackwood was eaten up with his own problems, whatever they were.

McClay watched from the dark shadows of an adjacent alley when Blackwood bombastically forced his way into the sheriff's office and strained his ears to catch the drift of what ensued.

The sounds of violence glazed his cold grey eyes with amazement. 'Waal, whadyuh know?' he breathed.

He scurried back to the Lucky Horseshoe and made urgent signs to Orson Rymer. Not many minutes later the gambler excused himself from his poker game and glided out to join McClay on a backyard path that meandered past stacks of empty crates to the privy.

McClay recounted all he had seen and heard.

Rymer bared his even white teeth in an evil grin. 'There's no fool like a jealous fool,' he said. 'It looks like things are coming to a head.'

He pulled a notebook from an inner pocket, wrote rapidly and tore off the sheet. He signed his handiwork simply 'R', folded it in four and shoved it into McClay's dirty, broken-nailed fingers.

'You're to ride back directly to the Double-B, McClay, and deliver this personally to Mrs Jessica Blackwood, you understand? Then come straight back here.'

'What's up, Rymer?' McClay said, bemused.

Rymer gave an ugly laugh as though relishing some secret and especially dirty jest. He knew the brutish McClay could neither read nor write and would be unable to learn anything from the paper he was to deliver for him.

'Tonight there could be other work needing your special skills, Snake.' He raised his hand as though it contained an invisible gun and crooked a long trigger finger meaningfully. 'You might even be able to write off the whole of your debt to me in one fell swoop.'

McClay nodded his misshapen head eagerly. His fringe of lank hair fell across his low brow and he moistened his grubby lips with an astonishingly pink tongue.

'That'd be damn' good, mister. Jest gimme the word.'

5

Temptress Jessica

Ross Kemp tugged off his boots, loosened his belt and laid his aching body on the cot in his office. Hand-to-hand combat with Boyd Blackwood had been like taking on a grizzly bear. It had tested all his strength.

But his bruises and split skin would heal and mend. On a physical level, a man could cope. It required not much better than a healthy metabolism, regular meals and sleep, and a steering-clear of dirt and infection.

The true test was something different again.

Into Kemp's muzzy head came the image of Ellen. Almost subconsciously, the awareness crept up on him once more that the aura of tranquillity that set her apart was under a dastardly threat.

He recognised that he was deeply troubled. Would Blackwood persist with his lunatic charges, even when sober? If he did, his stock with Ellen would tumble to rock-bottom. It brought him up with a start to realise just how much he valued her respect and good opinion.

He shook his head angrily, fearing Blackwood's punches had left him soft in the head. He had no business to be thinking of the girl – of any girl – in such a light. Like he'd often told Alec Tucker, his allegiance was owed to his job. It had to come first and last, and no decent man had any right to expect a woman to share the dangers and privations it posed. He could not wish them on anyone, least of all a beautiful girl set apart by her appealing qualities of unsullied youth and serenity.

In his disturbed thoughts, he found no place to remember that Ellen had already demonstrated, in the face of adversity at her old home, hidden reserves of courageous initiative and quiet fortitude. And he would have greeted with derision the suggestion that, if the truth were to be told, the seemingly reposed Ellen was reaching the end of her patience with his oh-so-brotherly interest in her well-being.

Kemp's mind ran from Ellen to her opposite – her stepmother, the darkly beautiful and somehow obviously dangerous Jessica. No wonder they'd not been able to live under the same roof! Where Ellen was restrained, Jessica was provoking. Though he was no puritan, her blatant attempts to procure his masculine attentions had annoyed him. He'd no desire to tangle with a married woman, even one as lushly desirable as Jessica.

Kemp wondered if Boyd Blackwood had observed his wife's flaunting of her mature charms. Maybe he suspected he, the sheriff, had or would reciprocate her interest, and that had triggered his wild notions.

'No, Mr Blackwood, your passionate wife's feminine wiles don't work on me,' he said aloud and sardonically.

This brought a grin to his stiffening face. But it froze, then was replaced by a frown of perplexity. An insistent yet light rapping on the thick pane set in the street door broke in on his wry amusement.

'Who's there?' he demanded.

'Jessica Blackwood. Please let me in, Mr Kemp!'

'Well, I'll be damned...' Kemp murmured under his breath.

Eyes narrowing, he figured out that maybe it wasn't so surprising. It was all part of the same business. He'd been thinking of the woman that very moment, sure, but it was because he had her husband in his cells – which was probably also why she was here.

For a second time in the same evening, he unlocked and unbolted the door.

Jessica gasped when she saw him. 'Mr Kemp! What's happened to you?'

He hesitated a moment, then answered her frankly, the fingertips of his left hand gently exploring the puffed contours of his face.

'This, ma'am, is the result of your husband's work.

She flinched at the bitterness in his voice.

Kemp stood aside, and she took it as an unspoken invitation to enter.

'Wh-why did Boyd do that?'

'I was hoping you could maybe enlighten me, Mrs Blackwood. He'd gotten some bee in his bonnet that you and me have been behaving – uh – unfittingly.'

She gazed at him apparently aghast, her amber eyes wide and lustrous. 'Oh! That really is too ridiculous!'

'You're not kidding. Them were my thoughts likewise. After he'd thrown his drunken weight around a mite, I tossed him in the calaboose to cool off. That's where he's staying till morning!'

Jessica's chin suddenly trembled and her head dipped.

'The beast! He's done it to spite me, I know!' There were tears in her eyes when she struggled to lift her head.

Embarrassed, Kemp turned and fiddled

with the wick in the oil lamp, brightening the dim light.

Jessica squared her shoulders. She tugged down the window blind, as though this decisive movement might help pull herself out of some emotional turmoil.

'Mr Kemp, please … I must talk to you in great confidence.' Her red lips quivered again. 'The fact is, I'm living a life of hell!'

Kemp swallowed and lifted his eyebrows at the vibrant words. This was a new Jessica Blackwood. Where was the poised, flirtatious woman who promenaded Main Street, dressed to leave no more than a speck to the imagination and making normally intelligent men slack-jawed and glassy-eyed?

Jessica's distress mounted. 'Boyd's absurd jealousies are too much! No one will ever know how miserable he has made me – how little he understands me.'

Kemp forced himself to remember that a God-fearing section of Cedar City society reckoned if rancher Blackwood understood his brazen young wife at all, he'd put her across his knee and give her a fanny-warming larruping. And maybe that's what she'd never had and needed.

She plunged on with her denunciation. 'He has so very little time for me, you know. He works sunup to sundown every day in the week. At b–, at *night*, he's too tired to – to talk. He takes his supper, then goes directly to sleep. A girl has no excitement at all. He denies me *friends*.'

Jessica pulled out a scrap of lace-fringed lawn and dabbed her eyes. Her bosom heaved.

Kemp could scarcely fail to be affected. Could any red-blooded male? But he had difficulty in finding words fair and appropriate to the situation.

He tentatively put a comforting hand to her shoulder. 'Now come along, Mrs Blackwood. You mustn't upset yourself. A fit and honest woman must look for contentment in her home and position. Self-pity won't solve no problems.'

'You're right, of course,' she said with a

catch in her voice. For a moment, she seemed to fight to get a grip of herself, but then she gave a fresh cry. 'Oh no… What can he have said about me? About you? He seems to think every man covets me…'

Her knees gave and she sank to the floor, sobbing half-hysterically.

'Here! You mustn't take on so!'

Kemp stooped awkwardly, and she seized his arm, he thought to raise herself to her feet. But she pulled him toward her with unexpected strength and he stumbled off balance onto his own knees and into her arms which she promptly wrapped around his neck, locking him in a tight embrace.

She whimpered against his chest, clinging to him impetuously and unreservedly.

Kemp's senses were intoxicated by the soft thrust of her female body against the hardening length of him.

'Don't–!' she pleaded. 'Don't push me away!'

Kemp had done no such thing, though he knew he had to. But the throaty plea was in itself incredibly seductive.

'Hey!' he said quickly. 'I don't think we ought to be doing this.' He scarcely knew what he was saying.

'Doing what, Sheriff? This?' Her lips sought out and were against his before he realised it.

A heady madness took hold of him as her deft fingers caressed and kneaded his broad shoulders, drawing him down with her to the floor. Her kiss was like an exquisite torture on his damaged lips. He was incapable of resistance.

He surrendered, and his own hands roamed unforgivably over her ripe body, exploring the secret, forbidden lushness of her. In response to her whispered urgings, he returned her drugging kiss and let his hungry lips wander downward to the throat she flung back and exposed to him.

It was when she attempted to entwine his legs with a probing, doeskin-booted foot that her toe inadvertently struck upon the painful bruise left on Kemp's shin by her husband's own solid riding boot.

Sanity returned to the sheriff with a rush. His face hot and his blue eyes ablaze with anguish, he struggled to extricate himself from her clutching embrace.

'God, no! This mustn't happen, you she-devil!' he jerked out.

Every bawdy, leering bar-room fantasy he'd ever heard disseminated about this woman rushed into his head to taunt him. Knowing her reputation and Boyd Blackwood's hate-filled jealousy, he'd been a crazy fool to let her step inside his office at this late hour.

He had to get her out – but fast!

'You forget yourself, ma'am,' he said harshly. 'That, or your morals are those of a saloon-girl!'

She tossed back the disordered, raven-black tresses from her face, and got to her own feet as he left her. Cheated of her conquest, she was white with repressed fury. Her amber eyes glinted with defiant passion.

To be rejected by a man was a new and galling experience for her. It was womenfolk who usually regarded her with censure. Their accusing looks were driven by envy, of course. Men always eyed her with admiration and bended to her will. And was it her fault that she was exciting and attractive? Most surely not. She couldn't help men losing their heads over a pretty woman. That, as Jessica saw it, was the way of the world.

'So!' she hissed. 'The high-and-mighty sheriff still has his principles, does he? Well, Mr Kemp, they give me a pain, and I shall encourage my husband to do his damnedest to ruin you!'

'Do what you will, Mrs Blackwood, but you'll not add my scalp to your belt. I find you a sorry picture of a woman – vain and self-seeking and inconsiderate of the conflict and unhappiness you cause.'

Jessica smoothed her hands over the rumples in her riding shirt, seething with impotent indignation at Kemp's perceptive tirade. Then with an explosive 'Tchah!' of disgust, she swung on her heel and wrenched open the door to the night and retreat.

But it afforded her a small, compensatory satisfaction that her mission hadn't been entirely in vain. Her personal wants hadn't been fulfilled, yet the fool sheriff was unaware she'd accomplished another important part of her object.

Let him believe he'd humiliated her. Before long he'd see the last laugh was hers!

Kemp felt sick to think how nearly Jessica had manoeuvred him into a situation that could clearly have compromised his whole position. He was tormented with self-disgust.

He returned to his bed, but bore the next hour in sleeplessness, critically re-examining where he stood. Again, Ellen came unbidden into his thoughts. Agonising doubts about the way he'd been toward her filled his head. But now he felt unclean and unworthy of the hints of interest she'd shown in him.

He couldn't bring himself to offer her a lawdog for a husband. But a disgraced lawdog, stripped of his office, would be an insult to her. He couldn't expect her to even look at him.

Moodily, Kemp wondered whether he'd gone wrong in making law enforcement his vocation. Take away the silver badge and he was a single man, never married, and probably could have made some woman a fine partner and provider. He was loyal and fair and honest. He was of an even-tempered disposition and had a dry sense of humour.

But now he had to ask himself, could he be faithful to a woman when he couldn't stay faithful to his own code?

The hands of the office clock went round and his dejection deepened. It wouldn't do. If his mind would give him no rest, he must give it work to occupy it to some profit. For starters, he could log Blackwood's arrest.

He got up, tucking his loosened shirt more tidily into the waistband of his pants.

Then he discovered his loss.

For a second he was disbelieving and felt and patted right around his belt.

Finally, a loose sigh escaped his lips.

'Damn the little hellcat!' he said. 'She's gone and stolen them.'

The bunch of keys which he'd had attached to a belt loop had gone missing.

He lit the lamp and looked carefully over the floor in a forlorn hope. But no, they'd vanished right enough. And among them were keys to the courthouse which adjoined the other side of the adobe jailhouse block.

It took Kemp several minutes to hunt up a duplicate key kept hidden at the back of a desk drawer.

Jaw clenched angrily, nerves taut as piano wires, he unlocked the solid oak door, but he knew before he got in to check the cells that Boyd Blackwood would be gone.

6

Murder from Ambush

Boyd Blackwood rode the wide trail for the Double-B at a fast canter. Every thud of the steeldust roan's hoofs sent a jarring pain shooting up his spine to his aching head.

The moon hung like a lantern high in the black velvet sky, surrounded by a dust-swirl of countless stars and tipping with silver the indigo bulk of the mountains that rimmed the horizon.

Every now and then Blackwood would utter an audible cuss that betrayed the fevered train of his thoughts. Freed from the jail by a remorseful Jessica, who had pleaded exhaustion from the late ride into town and was now resting up overnight at the Cedar City House, his one over-riding design was a crushing vengeance on the corrupting sheriff of Cedar City!

On the morrow, tidied up and recovered from his ordeal, he would ride out with bodyguards to go calling on Judge Franklin Ward. He would see to it the judge tore off Ross Kemp's badge and called new elections.

After news of Kemp's infamy had spread around, he plotted a rougher justice. There were some tough hombres on his payroll. That Snake McClay, for instance. Give them the word, and the once-popular Kemp would be not only out of his job, but out of town on a rail.

Blackwood wetted wind-dried lips. Even dead maybe…

The trail led through a grove of cottonwoods where at this season a stream trickled between the smoothly-worn rocks of a ford. The tall trees cut out most of the moonlight, making it a place of deep and possibly treacherous shadows for a horseman.

Just how treacherous, Blackwood didn't guess.

But knowing the need for care, he pulled at the reins of his lathered bronc. The obedient beast slackened its pace, throwing up its head with a jingle of bit-pieces and snorting heavily through distended nostrils. Then it whinnied and seemed reluctant to proceed into the darkness at all.

Blackwood snarled and slapped impatiently at its rump.

'Get going, you ornery critter!'

The baulky horse clop-clopped into the shadows of the trees. It clattered over boulders etched with the silver flashes of the splashing stream.

Blackwood grunted his satisfaction at the cautious and successful passage. He prodded the roan with his spurred heels and felt the great beast surge forward under his hard-clamped thighs.

As they broke out of the blackness under the trees, the silhouette of horse and rider was stark against the light of the moon. An easy target for the dry-gulcher left behind, crouched in the cover of the cottonwoods.

He raised his Winchester to his shoulder, levering a shell into the breech. He squeezed the trigger and the spiteful snap of the rifle's fire split the night's silence.

The heavy .44 slug smashed the life out of the rancher, toppling him lifeless from the saddle with nary a cry.

Blackwood's startled steeldust roan plunged on, dragging its dead rider, till his foot dislodged itself from the stirrup.

The horse circled in confusion before it came back to the fallen man. It put its soft nose to the back of his neck exploring the prone body, unaware of the significance of the ugly crimson stain spreading in the middle of Blackwood's suit-coated back.

When it scented the blood, it gave a whinny of fear and moved off.

Sheriff Kemp shook the coffee pot that sat on the still-warm iron of the pot-bellied office stove. The dregs of his last brew sloshed about in the bottom and he poured them into an enamelled mug. He winced when his mouth filled with the strong black liquid.

A bitter cup for a bitter man.

From a high shelf, he hauled down a stout ledger, half-bound in leather. This was his jailhouse logbook. In it, entered in his bold, firm hand, were largely the names of rowdy cowhands who'd let off their steam in ways unacceptable to their fellow men. If the law was to be administered fairly in Cedar City, without favour, Kemp owed it to this roll of minor miscreants that he should add the line 'Boyd Blackwood, rancher, drunk and disorderly'.

He was beholden, by oath of office. It was his responsibility to take out after Blackwood and escort him back to the cells. Or at the very least, to enforce the local statute that obliged him to impose and collect a fine. Payment of the same should have been a condition of the rancher's release.

Neglect to perform this duty, and Kemp hated to think what scurrilous story would go the rounds, especially if it became known

Blackwood's delectable wife had been involved in the matter…

In a grim frame of mind, he fastened on his gun rig and took down his saddle gun, a Winchester .44, from the wall rack. He'd no doubt Blackwood would have headed directly for the shelter of his ranch, probably in some haste to elude ignominious re-arrest.

The night air sharpened the edges of Kemp's bleak fury on the trail to the Double-B. He rode automatically, preoccupied. It still stuck in his craw to think he'd been bamboozled. Played for a sucker. And the manner of it was belittling. He was no better than the uncouth riff-raff, typified by the beef-prodder pair Lew and Max, whose ogling eyes went out on stalks as they lusted after Jessica Blackwood.

The upright officer of the law had been put to the acid test and proved as fallible as the common herd.

But he had no stomach for laying even his legal hands on his temptress. Right now he was impatient to take up the argument with Boyd Blackwood.

The trail rounded a ridged outcrop of the hills, surmounted by a cluster of oaks growing some thirty-five feet above the road. A froth of clouds drifted across the moon. Ridge and cloud cast blotches of blackness in Kemp's path, but he was gifted with quick adaption to night vision and he spurred his mount on at an unfaltering pace that presently brought him to the still-deeper shadows of the cottonwood grove.

Splashing through the stream, Kemp saw the form of a man sprawled on the trail ahead. Boyd Blackwood?

Kemp drew rein and laid his hand in a gentle pat on the neck of his horse. 'This looks bad,' he said quietly. 'Better get down.'

He swung out of the saddle and crouched beside the inert body, tilting back his stetson. It was indeed Blackwood. Kemp's breath was exhaled in a low whistle.

'Shot, by God!'

Sticky blood was congealing around the

bullet wound in the centre of Blackwood's back. He was clearly dead, but Kemp had difficulty in grasping that his erstwhile prisoner, and the richest man in the county, would walk no more. Blackwood was a sturdily-built, muscular man, set apart by the aggression and vitality that had driven him to material success. His death seemed unthinkable.

Almost in reflex, Kemp took off his hat.

But the opportunity to come to terms with the staggering turn of events was denied the sheriff.

Engrossed in his thoughts and the always-sobering horror of a murdered corpse, Kemp didn't hear the stealthy footfalls behind him. He only started to turn when a sudden swishing noise alerted him. The bushwhacker had been lying in wait! He saw no more than a blur of movement before the butt of a revolver slammed into his temple.

Kemp's world exploded in a swirling blaze of stars, rapidly succeeded by inky, redshot darkness.

He fell across the dead rancher, unconscious.

Chilly water was splashing over Kemp's face when he opened his eyes.

'Ugh!' he spluttered. 'What's going on?'

'Give the stinkin' lawdog some more!' said a voice he recognised as Jeremiah McClay's.

'Ain't got no more, Snake. Canteen's empty,' said another Double-B hand.

A boot-cap kicked Kemp in the ribs experimentally. He blinked and looked around him, though his head hurt intolerably. He was lying on his back at the side of the trail some miles back toward Cedar City where it curved round the distinctive oak-topped ridge. He was surrounded by four of Blackwood's range crew, including Snake McClay.

He fingered his forehead gingerly, discovering an egg-like swelling. Coherent thoughts began to trickle back into his numbed brain.

'Who brought me here?' he struggled to say. Every word was a sliver of sheer agony that sent reeling echoes through his head. 'What have you done with Blackwood?'

McClay sneered. 'Ain't much left to be done 'cept plant 'im. Yuh saw to that, yuh back-shootin' bastard! Too bad yore cayuse threw yuh as yuh came back lickety-spit aroun' the curve!'

Kemp heaved himself up onto his elbows and glared in amazement at the runty gunslick. The effort sent his head hammering like a piston in a steam engine.

'Blackwood was bushwhacked – shot with a rifle, looked like.'

'Don't we know it!' McClay said.

Another cowpoke stepped forward, waving the familiar shape of Kemp's own Winchester. 'I took the liberty of gettin' yore saddle-gun outa the scabbard, Mr Sheriff,' he said with scornful derision. 'The barrel's fouled an' it smells jest like it's bin fired in the last half-hour.'

'Hell's teeth! You think I killed your boss?'

'Damned right we do, Kemp,' McClay cut in. 'I seen yuh ride outa town jest after

Blackwood left. Real proddy an' in an all-fired hurry.'

Kemp's eyes slitted. 'What an ex-con believes won't count for much.'

The shrewd comment caught McClay by surprise, flicking him on the raw.

'That's over an' done, Kemp,' he snarled back. ''Sides, the evidence ain't mine. The boys here came out from the Double-B an' found the boss' body where yuh caught up an' shot 'im down. Then they rode on toward town an' found yuh here, where yuh'd taken a tumble an' knocked yuhself stupid. After that, I came along an' we pieced together what yuh did, yuh dirty murderer!'

'I wouldn't shoot a citizen dead in cold blood!' Kemp protested.

McClay gave a stained-toothed grin. 'Reck'n we'll let the court decide that, Kemp. We're takin' yuh in. Git up an' on yore hoss!'

The puncher with the Winchester growled. 'Ain't no secret there was a grudge between you an' Blackwood, Kemp. Seems like folks in town is sayin' you been carryin' on with his wife an' all. Blackwood was vowin' to fix you. Waal, you got to him first, I guess!'

Kemp lurched to his feet and the world swayed but he managed not to fall. He had to allow that what the cow-hand said about Blackwood and himself must have made good whiskey talk up and down Main Street. He'd tangled publicly with the rancher, and everyone had heard Blackwood swear revenge.

He wondered just how much had been said behind his back. It looked like things could be pretty black for him when they hit town. With Blackwood's death and the accusations of the Double-B men hanging over him, one clear certainty in his dazed mind was that he'd have to turn in his badge. As the cowhand had threatened, he might even have to stand trial.

He'd had cause and opportunity to kill Blackwood. And he had no alibi.

Unaccountably, the prospect of his removal from office brought him relief, almost as though deep inside he'd already acknowledged he was unfit and reluctant to continue shouldering the burden.

'But someone must've killed Blackwood,' he said aloud. 'I've got to see my deputy. He'll have to organise a search, a posse–'

'Drop it, mister,' one of the Double-B riders said. 'We got you dead to rights. There ain't gonna be no flamin' *posse.*' He finished with a contemptuous oath that said what could be done with that.

McClay gloated. 'Jeez, Kemp I'd sure hate to be in yore shoes. They'll mebbe dangle yuh from a neck-rope fer this!'

The gravity of his predicament began to register. He had been put on the spot by a person or persons unknown.

Much would hinge on the thinking of the town. Though it hadn't seemed too important before, he realised that Jessica had somehow contrived to put a stigma on his character, although he'd always rebuffed her blatant attempts to flirt with him.

Surely, now her husband had been

murdered, she would speak up and at least scotch the suggestion he'd been involved in some kind of affair with her.

A solid hand fell roughly on Kemp's shoulder.

'Get on your horse, *Sheriff,* and I'll mount up behind and look after you.' The speaker sniggered. 'We wouldn't want anythin' else to happen to you before you're safely locked up in one of them cells of your'n.'

McClay gave an ugly laugh. 'We don't want the sheriff's hoss runnin' away ag'in, do we, fellers? That'd be too bad!'

Kemp's horse was brought over from where the Double-B men had found it grazing unconcernedly nearby. Kemp put his foot in the stirrup, noticing for the first time that the reassuring bulk of his Colt had already been removed from his right thigh.

He was a prisoner.

7

Sheriff on Trial

The news of Boyd Blackwood's killing and the accusing of Sheriff Ross Kemp spread through Cedar City like a prairie fire. As a preliminary to a trial, an inquest was held and the county coroner found that Boyd Blackwood had met his death as the result of a shot fired from a rifle, to wit, a .44 calibre Winchester, and Ross Kemp was charged with his murder.

Silently, Kemp endured the insult of being locked up in what he'd thought of as his own jail. Alec Tucker, officially promoted and confirmed as Sheriff of Cedar City, was apologetic.

'I have to keep yuh in the cooler, all legal-like, Ross, but I'll see to it you're fed good grub, an' the bunk can't be no worse than that ol' cot of yours.'

Tucker also loyally reported back on what was being said outside.

Blackwood's widow, it transpired, was making no attempt to cool the heated tongue-wagging. A junior clerk who worked for Isaac Siebert leaked the information that Jessica was only biding a respectable time for grieving before denouncing Kemp as her husband's sworn enemy and killer.

It was whispered the widow would be the star witness at Kemp's coming trial and would be making startling revelations about the ex-sheriff.

Kemp was devastated. 'That can't be true!' he said to Tucker.

The new sheriff shook his head sadly. 'Wicked, ain't it? The lies a spurned woman'll tell.'

'There must be more to it than that...' Kemp scratched his head and paced his cell.

He dredged from his memory everything he knew or had ever heard told about the

Blackwoods. Naturally, most of it seemed to have no real bearing on a murder, and he dismissed it as irrelevant. But a couple of unpromising scraps nagged persistently round the edges of his reasoning.

First, there was the clandestine meeting Ellen had witnessed between Jessica and the gambler Orson Rymer. He'd formerly regarded a liaison between them as being none of his business. With his circumstances dramatically changed, that might no longer be the case.

Kemp's vague suspicion was further stirred by the second mystery, presented to him by Blackwood himself in the course of his absurd allegations on the night of his death. Blackwood had been upset to the extent of going on a drunken spree about secret notes sent to his wife and signed with an initial that had been his, the sheriff's.

What had that initial been? 'K' for Kemp or 'R' for Ross?

And if it had been 'R' might it not just as easily have stood for Rymer?

‘Alec!’ Kemp yelled. ‘Come here!’

Tucker appeared in the jailhouse doorway, puzzled. ‘What’s the hollerin’ for, Ross?’

Kemp explained, and Tucker shook his head sceptically. ‘Sounds like clutchin’ at straws, ol’ buddy. But I’ll do what yuh ask an’ ask around. Must say, it’s always had me beat what’s kept that slicker Rymer in a cowtown like Cedar City.’

Kemp’s hopes were dashed in the scant matter of a few hours.

Tucker left willing, but came back to the jailhouse scowling.

‘Sorry, it’s no dice, Ross. Rymer couldna killed Blackwood. He spent the whole of that night – before and after yuh was chasin’ Blackwood – at the Lucky Horseshoe. I got several honest, poker-playin’ citizens to swear as how he was busy lightenin’ their pockets an’ stuffin’ his own!’

‘He must’ve slipped out sometime and come back.’

‘Yeah … twice. But only long enough to excuse hisself to go to the privy.’

Kemp nodded woodenly. 'All right. Thanks, Alec.'

He was a man accustomed to action, to seizing the initiative and using it to best effect. Delegation had never come easy to him during his period of office. Now, organising his defence from the narrow confines of three adobe walls and an iron grille was a task demonstrably beyond him.

His agitation deepened and his spirits sank. He began to imagine the whole sorry mess might be his comeuppance for being less than square with Ellen Blackwood. Or his needings for falling into the tempting embrace of Jessica Blackwood.

The five days before the trial were the longest in Kemp's life. Sunup on the sixth morning found him unable to face the breakfast Tucker brought him of freshly brewed coffee, flapjacks and ham and eggs.

'I'll just take the java,' Kemp said. 'The sooner this thing gets done with the better.'

Tucker met his eyes momentarily, then very purposefully looked away. 'Mebbe it'd be best if there was a breakout,' he mumbled. 'I c'd git kinda careless an' yuh might cut an' run.'

Kemp brushed the proposition aside. 'Then you'd be in trouble, too. Right up to your gullet. Forget it.'

Unlike Tucker, more than anybody in Cedar City, he was incapable of accepting that truth wouldn't prevail in the end. His basic honesty and belief in the forces of right acted against him in this. He just couldn't envisage the bizarre chain of evidence holding together against him. Though the experience was going to be harrowing, he still thought the murder charge he faced had to be thrown out.

The courtroom was packed. Every one of the high, barred windows had been opened for maximum ventilation, but an oppressive fug rose about the tightly filled wooden benches set out for the agog public of Cedar City. Smoking was in no way prohibited. Pipes and cheroots and cigarettes collaborated with sweaty bodies to produce a visible stench that rose in coiling wreaths to the rafters.

Humanity proved it stank before a word was spoken. And the stage was set for the primitive legal system of this frontier community to do the same.

At the front of the room, a long table stood on a dais. Judge Franklin Ward was installed in a high-backed chair at the table, facing the benches. He peered myopically over *pince-nez* eye-glasses at the papers scattered before him. His beaky nose gave him a bird-like appearance and wings of fluffy white hair stood out from the side of his head above pointy ears. A limp flag bearing the Stars and Stripes of the American States was draped at an angle across the wall behind his head.

Sitting behind a long, narrow table to the judge's right, was an all-male jury of eleven.

Sheriff Alec Tucker escorted his former boss down the centre aisle to a bench set at the judge's left and stood behind him.

A rumble of avid conversation broke out on the public benches at Ross Kemp's entry.

Judge Ward took up a gavel in a wrinkled, arthritic hand and hammered astonishingly hard on his table, setting the water in a glass pitcher quivering with concentric ripples. There was a jingle of spur dangles, a scrape of boots and a rustle of clothing as everybody present stood up.

'Court in session!' The word was given; Kemp's trial was on.

The judge tapped again with the wooden hammer, and there was more shuffling as citizens, jurors and accused sat down.

The clerk of the court, who in everyday life was the ancient barkeep at the Lucky Horseshoe, cleared his throat noisily before reading out the count of murder against Ross Kemp. It alleged he did discharge into the back of Boyd Blackwood with intent a .44 calibre rifle.

A new buzz of excitement ran through the assembly. Judge Ward clicked his teeth together in stern disapproval and wielded his gavel a third time.

'Order! Order, or I'll clear the courtroom!'

When near-silence was restored, the assistant county attorney stepped forward in to the space before the dais and began the case for the prosecution. A series of witnesses was called whose testimony rapidly established the bad blood that had existed between the sheriff Kemp and the rancher Blackwood.

Kemp, who had elected to conduct his own defence, didn't bother to cross-examine. 'All this stuff is incontrovertible. I'll not contest the witnesses' detail,' he advised the judge.

Then the prosecutor called for his star witness.

The bow-legged clerk straightened to his feet.

'Call Mrs Jessica Blackwood!'

Heads swivelled and necks craned. Gasps and sighs greeted the widow's entrance. She was in weeds, but the black garments and veil, whether by virtue of their cut or the wearer's shapeliness, made a mockery of mourning, heightening her sexuality.

Something welled up for a large number of the male onlookers. They would have said it was sympathy. Judge Ward's crippled old fingers adjusted his glasses, then strayed to his throat to straighten his cravat.

Jessica was accompanied by the Blackwood lawyer, Isaac Siebert. Although the widow walked tall and erect, he had one hand at her elbow as if he feared she might suddenly be prostrated by grief without the support. Siebert's other nervous hand clasped a black stovepipe hat and he wore a rusty-black clawhammer coat. Beneath the goatee beard that tufted his chin, a string tie was knotted under a stiff white shirt collar.

Jessica placed a slim hand on a Bible and took the oath. She then took the witness stand and Siebert an empty, reserved seat at the front of the public benches, mopping his brow with a large handkerchief and looking highly uncomfortable. Before he sat down he flashed a look at the unwashed populace and another at Ross Kemp. Both were furtive.

The prosecutor, showing an excess of solicitousness, modulated his voice to draw out Jessica's testimony. Into the hushed room, she dropped the quiet words that totally damned Ross Kemp.

'Yes, Mr Kemp had been – bothering me with his attentions,' she agreed.

'And in what form did the accused couch these – er – attentions?'

'Notes! He sent disgraceful notes.'

This tallied with testimony from other witnesses to whom Blackwood had admitted his anger at discovering secret correspondence to his wife.

Judge Ward leaned forward expectantly and interjected. 'The notes,' he wheezed, his watery eyes shining. 'I want to read them. Do we have them as exhibits?'

The clerk of the court bobbed up. 'If it please your honour, the notes have not been presented.'

The white-haired jurist looked over his glasses at Jessica, frowning his reproof. 'What has become of the prisoner's notes?'

The audience stirred.

Jessica fluttered her eyelashes and dropped her head. She bit her lip. It was all very heart-melting.

'I destroyed them, Judge,' she said. 'I retrieved them from my husband's breast pocket and burned them. They weren't just embarrassing. They had caused my husband's death. They were *evil.*'

A subdued murmur of assent ran through the stuffy room, and Kemp observed Judge Ward visibly back off, nodding his bird-like head. 'Of course, of course,' the old cuss muttered.

Kemp rose to cross-examine Jessica. His face was set in hard, frozen lines, masking his fury. He looked out over the packed benches. Only one person gave him what could have been construed as a look of sympathy. That was Ellen Blackwood. The rest gazed back in curiosity or plain hostility.

'Mrs Blackwood, if there's anything evil about this case, it's your heart,' he began. 'What you've told this court is a pack of wicked lies–'

The prosecutor leaped to his feet, objecting.

'The prisoner is intimidating the witness, your honour! I insist he limits himself to asking material questions.'

'Upheld,' the judge intoned. 'Kemp, I forbid you to hector the witness. Regardless of the gravity of your position, I insist you show proper respect and feeling for a bereaved woman.'

Hamstrung, Kemp fumblingly tried to take issue with Jessica in a series of ineffective questions. Impassively, she denied everything his enquiries implied with flat monosyllables inaudible beyond the jury and the front row of the public benches.

Folk at the back of the courtroom stood up, the better to savvy the drift of the interchange, till the judge rapped with his gavel and warned them anyone disturbing the proceedings would be summarily thrown out.

Kemp was appalled at Jessica's glibness; Isaac Siebert, whom he suspected knew things not being said, looked more uneasy than she did, his chin beard twitching spasmodically with the trembling of his jaw.

Dully, Kemp realised his position was desperate. After Jessica was released from the stand, it was all anti-climax.

Judge Ward summed it up for the jury. 'The prisoner had powerful motives and clear opportunity. He faced disgrace and loss of office. He comes before us due only to his own recklessness. Spurring his horse back to Cedar City hell for leather in the moonglow, he was unseated and undone. The testimony so bravely given by the unfortunate widow and the other witnesses, the proof of the firing of the sheriff's Winchester – these things are positive indicators of guilt.'

Mindful of a rumbling belly, the judge decreed the jury should retire and the courtroom be cleared for a dinner break. 'Refreshments can be sent into the jury during the course of their deliberations, which I trust shall not be protracted.'

An hour later the court reconvened. Again, the room was packed to hot overflowing to see the outcome of the sensation that had rocked Cedar City.

Judge Ward rapped for order and the gabbling ceased.

His honour addressed the foreman of the jury. 'I understand you've reached a finding.'

Ross Kemp swallowed hard as he scanned the faces of the eleven whose word held his destiny. They ranged from bank cashier to cowhand. Bearded or shaven, office-pale or range-bronzed, each face shone with sweat; each juror sat stiffly.

The foreman, a mournful gent with a drooping, tobacco-yellowed moustache who ran a saddle and harness shop, shuffled to his feet.

'We have, your honour. We find the accused guilty, but make a strong recommendation for mercy in consideration of his previous unblemished record and his years of service as a law officer.'

The room went into uproar as the spectators vigorously debated amongst themselves the merits of the verdict and the jury's rider.

'Order! Order!'

It took the united efforts of the judge and the clerk of the court to quell the bedlam.

Judge Ward thanked the jury for their work and the benefit of their opinions. 'In the light and wisdom of judicial experience, I can confirm that you have returned the only possible verdict.'

Kemp knew that the good people of Cedar City would also acknowledge that the jury had done their best for him in what were near-impossible circumstances.

His eyes sought out Ellen. She looked strained and white-faced, but maybe, too, a little relieved. Mercy would mean, at the very least, that he wouldn't hang. Yet surely the outcome couldn't matter a whole lot to her in her own black mourning clothes. Kemp remained expressionless but his guts were wrenched by the injustice. For all she knew, he was the rogue who'd had impure designs on her stepmother and had shot her father, wasn't he?

There was now only one more question, which Judge Ward decided without ado.

'Ross Kemp, I sentence you to ten years in the state penitentiary.'

8

Blackwood's Will

Ross Kemp was hustled aboard a train, locked up in a smelly freight car like an animal in a cage. It was like even the pair deputed to ride shotgun on him preferred to have him out of sight as soon as possible.

The whole damned town was down on him. Even those – mostly womenfolk – who had no time for Jessica Blackwood, had listened to the shameless bitch's lies, hypocritically finding prurient relish in his dishonour. The Cedar City populace had followed his circus of a trial with awful fascination but now wanted nothing more to do with its fallen hero.

'It's over with … get him out of our sight,' they might have said.

At the junction of the spur line that served the cowtown, Kemp was delivered into the keeping of prison guards sent to collect him.

He was incarcerated in a closed, plank-sided, windowless wagon that was in effect a box on wheels and taken to the grim, stone-built fortress of the penitentiary. Here his clothes, noisome from the mode of his transport, were taken away and he was rigged out in striped convict's garb little cleaner.

They also took away his name and reduced his identity to a six-digit number.

His bug-ridden cell was to be shared with a train robber called Seamus Maloney who never stopped bragging – about his strength, his marksmanship, the women he'd bedded, the bets he'd won, the loot he'd taken. According to Maloney, the notorious gang led by his brother had brought dynamiting trains to a fine art and was the terror of the Middle West.

Kemp soon recognised the habit of mendacious self-promotion was Maloney's way of bolstering his courage in this soul-destroying place. Maloney craved company and talk like a backwoodsman making out miles from civilisation.

Occasionally, Maloney asked questions, but Kemp was not to be drawn. Maloney accepted his new cell-mate's taciturnity without resentment. 'To be sure, seein's it's nothin' you'd be havin' to say at all, at all, let miself tell you about the time 'twas when I…' And so he would grab the chance to brag some more.

The fit prisoners spent their days in work gangs, out under the blazing sun, breaking rocks. Besides rocks, swinging the heavy sledges was also seen by the authorities as a way of breaking any spirit of rebellion that might linger in their charges.

The guards watched over the punishing activity with carbines draped over bent arms. No let-up was allowed. No talking. No singing. Just the grueling work in the blistering heat.

One night, about two weeks after Kemp's arrival, Maloney told him about visiting day.

They'd been returned to their cell from the dining-hall and Maloney had lit the solitary candle.

''Tis every fourth Sunday I'll be tellin' you, an' t'morrer's the day. Sure 'twill be no surprise to miself if you'll be havin' folks a-droppin' by.'

'Nope. The place I was at ain't got time for a convicted murderer. I'll not be having no visitors.'

'Miself neither,' Maloney said. 'I'll be havin' you know it's a forgotten man you–'

'Lights out!' a warder's harsh voice bellowed, and Maloney's sounding-off was postponed.

After Maloney had blown out the candle, Kemp huddled in his musty blankets. Like he'd said, he was certain everyone in Cedar City had abandoned him. Renegade lawmen were a shameful disgrace to a community.

The eerie white light of a full moon shining through the barred window heightened Kemp's feeling that he was no longer part of a real world. The next ten years were to be a living death, during which he would be crushed, and ground and destroyed as surely as the rocks he smashed each day.

Then the anger started to bubble within him, swiftly coming to a boil. He wanted to yell and rage. *'I'm innocent – innocent, you fools!'*

In his short time here, he'd already seen prisoners crack and bang their crazy skulls against the stone walls before they were dragged away by the jeering guards to solitary confinement or worse. He hoped he could stay strong enough not to resort to such imbecile futility himself.

His one silent prayer was that at least Ellen Blackwood would know in the depth of her good heart that he'd faced a trumped-up charge and was the victim of a cynically calculated frame-up.

'Visitor for Prisoner 679135! Move, will yuh!'

The warder turned the heavy key in the

lock of the cell door and pushed Kemp out at the point of his carbine.

Kemp grunted and shambled into the bleak corridor.

'Sure, it's a foine thing, you'll not deny – a visitor *unexpected,* you sly dog!' Maloney teased. 'A handsome woman, I'll be bound!'

But Kemp was genuinely surprised to find no mistake had been made. Seated behind the barred grille waiting to see him was Ellen Blackwood!

His heart leaped. In this instant, he knew at last that the girl mustn't believe he'd cold-bloodedly murdered her father.

One of her small, smooth hands crept to her throat, clutching the strings of her black bonnet. Though he didn't guess it, she was shocked by his changed appearance. The injustice he'd suffered and the rigours of life in the pen had already hollowed his cheeks and stooped his broad shoulders. And his once-blue eyes had taken on a leaden look.

He managed a smile of sorts. 'Hullo, Miss Ellen. I'm right glad to see you.'

She coloured a little. 'I hope you don't mind my coming.'

'Mind! It's the answer to my prayer that you've come, though I find it shaming that an honest young woman like yourself should have to step within these walls.'

He responded with an intensity Ellen had never heard from him before. That was a measure in itself of his changed circumstances. But also, still there, was the same rough honesty and openness that had always appealed to her in him.

'I had to come. To let you know that my faith in you stands, that I'll never be able to believe you committed the terrible crime you've been imprisoned for.'

Her hazel eyes filled and glistened, so that Kemp longed to tear down the barrier between them with his bare hands. But he knew that the strongest thing he could do was not give way to his powerful emotions.

'I got to think of some way to prove my innocence and restore my honour, Miss Ellen,' he said, clenching his fists so that the torn nails gouged the work-blistered palms. 'To get out of here and hunt down the devils who really did kill your father. There's been a conspiracy of some kind, that I'm sure.'

Ellen fidgeted uncomfortably on the hard wooden chair. 'My stepmother lied, of course.' She let go a trembling sigh. 'Since you were – taken away, other disturbing things have come to light that I think affect her. It's possible they have a connection with her despicable conduct, yet I hardly know what I should do...'

'You can start by telling me, Miss Ellen. It'll get it off your chest is all, I guess. But it could – just *could* resolve my own suspicions.'

Ellen clasped both hands in her lap and thoughtfully began her story.

Kemp listened, and a sinking sensation claimed the pit of his stomach. Jessica had automatically inherited the rich Double-B holdings as Blackwood's widow. But Ellen was far from sure this was in accordance with her father's last wishes.

'You remember pa's old housekeeper, Mrs Martha Dunbar?'

'Indeed I do, Miss Ellen. And her husband Hank, that stove-up waddy your pa kept on to do chores around the home-lot.'

Ellen nodded 'Those are the people. A grand old pair. After I left the Double-B and came to town to live, Mrs Dunbar kept in touch with me.' Ellen's eyes fell to her restless hands. 'Mrs Dunbar said I favoured my mother a lot, and her memory was precious. She also had little time for Jessica.'

'Many of the smarter Cedar City women-folk hadn't. Her manner spelled trouble.'

A smile tugged at Ellen's lips. 'Mrs Dunbar said her name should have been Jezebel, not Jessica.'

'She weren't far wrong,' Kemp said soberly.

'Maybe the prejudice coloured the story Mrs Dunbar has told me, but the facts speak for themselves and are disturbing nonetheless.'

Ellen paused, as though still uncertain

that she should burden the ex-sheriff, before plunging on. 'Mr Kemp, Mrs Dunbar maintains that Jessica, though father's widow, has inherited the Double-B illegally. On the evening before his death, pa drew up a new will, and Mrs Dunbar and her husband put their marks on it as witnesses.'

'Lord sakes! Do the Dunbars know what it said?'

'Only a broad idea. They're both illiterate, you see.'

'Yeah, I see.'

'So they couldn't read the paper they signed. But Mrs Dunbar says she assumed "Jezebel" was being cut out due to what father said was her alley-catting with – with you!'

'The hell with it! Them damned notes again!'

'Exactly. Father said Jessica's infidelity was proven by the notes you'd writ her.'

'I didn't write no notes.'

'No, but someone did, and father vowed to deposit the new will with his lawyer, and to "settle your hash" as he put it.'

For several seconds Ellen and Kemp stared at each other in silence. Finally, Kemp shook his head. 'This doesn't make sense. Why hasn't Isaac Siebert produced that will? Has he spoken to you about it?'

'He hasn't. The will that was read in Mr Siebert's office following father's death was one drawn up several years ago, after the occasion of his second marriage.'

'You've mentioned Mrs Dunbar's story to the lawyer, maybe?'

'Yes. And Mr Siebert denied receiving any such document. But I thought there was something a mite odd about his manner.'

Kemp recalled Isaac Siebert's shifty demeanour at the trial. It tied in. Dirty work had been afoot ... and the shyster had known it!

'I figure the sonofabitch could tell us a whole lot more than he's letting on,' he choked. 'It sure riles a man being cooped up in here. Ten years!'

Ellen flinched at his pent-up rage.

'I'm sorry if I've added to your troubles, Mr Kemp.'

Kemp observed her distress and took hold of himself, determining not to dwell on the topic of his imprisonment. When he spoke again, he said, 'Don't fret yourself. I want to know what's happening in Cedar City now I've been put away. Keep me posted on Siebert. Also, I want to keep up with your father's widow – what she's doing and who she sees.'

Ellen drew a quick breath. 'That reminds me of another thing I have to tell you. About that gambler man who appears to have taken up residence at the hotel.'

'Orson Rymer?' Kemp said directly, attentively. 'I've always thought the scum had his finger in this pie somehow. Ever since you told me about him meeting Jessica on the sly.'

'He's seeing her openly now,' Ellen said with a rush, fearful of re-awakening Kemp's agitation. 'The scoundrel is unconscionable. He's a frequent visitor to the Double-B.

Comforting Mrs Blackwood in her bereavement, he's told the hotel workers.'

'That figures, too,' Kemp remarked. 'The notes that got your pa fired up were signed: "R". For Rymer, I reckoned. But Deputy Tucker found out Rymer had a solid alibi for the time of the murder which like knocked the guts outa that idea.'

'Time's up!' barked the voice of a prison guard behind him.

Ellen abruptly looked pale and small and scared.

This was an unhappy spell for her, too, Kemp realised. He burned to ask if she'd visit him again in four Sundays' time, but the dilemma seemed crazily familiar. It wasn't right and proper to expect a desirable girl like Ellen Blackwood to take an interest in a man like himself. No longer because he was sheriff and all, but because he was branded a murderer – a convict with no hope of release for ten years.

'I'm powerful obliged for all you've told me, Miss Ellen,' he began.'You must–'

Another guttural voice broke in. 'Get that prisoner back to the cells, warder!'

The guard behind him clapped his hand roughly on his shoulder and tugged. 'You heard, feller!'

'Goodbye, Miss Ellen. And thank you again.'

He had a last brief glimpse of brimming eyes. 'Take care, Mr Kemp!' she struggled to say. Then he was pitched through an open door back into the numbing horror of his spartan prison life.

Kemp looked haggard when he was returned to his cell.

Maloney clucked his tongue. ''Tis bad news you've been hear-r-rin' of, is it not?'

'Never mind, never mind,' Kemp said curtly, waving a dismissive hand.

He slumped onto his bunk and clasped his throbbing head. All he'd learned span in taunting review through his troubled mind.

'That'd be right now. Set your good self down for a spell,' said his garrulous cell-mate, forever strong on giving advice. 'Sure an' I was after-r tellin' before how 'twas when me an' me brother was told how our poor-r-r mother, who was the foinest woman as ever drew breath…'

But Kemp wasn't listening to a word. Silently, inevitably the resolve to escape, or die in the attempt, hardened within him.

He'd had his gutsful of the pen.

9

'Not More Killing, Please!'

Jessica Blackwood paced the room that had been her husband's office in the big rock-and-adobe ranch-house of the Double-B. A cool breeze wafted through the open windows, carrying the rhythmic *clank-clank* of the steadily turning vanes of a windmill. From across the broad sweep of the yard, a small chorus of work sounds was contributed by those labouring in the whitewashed cookhouse, barns and smithy.

Despite Boyd Blackwood's death, the rich spread's life went on for the present with the forceful momentum he'd lent it. Closer at hand, within the room, his presence lingered in the deer-head mounted on the wall above the fireplace and the bearskin rug on the floor.

Jessica's dark hair was parted at the centre and drawn severely to a bun at her nape. As a concession to mourning, her full skirt was black, but her loose bodice was white and frilled and there were sandals on her bare feet.

None of this garb made her feel comfortable. Things were weighing heavily on her mind. The sweet fruit of her wealthy widowhood, she'd rapidly discovered, was rotten at the core.

A rapping of heavy knuckles on the door interrupted Jessica's contemplation, and the door was thrust open before she could answer. She ran a cold glance over the woman who intruded on her privacy.

'Mrs Dunbar! What is this?'

'It's enough, ma'am, an' more. Me an' Hank are quittin' this same day!'

The two women stood face to face, feet apart, but worlds and a generation yawned between them. Martha Dunbar was a barrel-shaped, grey-haired woman with a steely glint in her eye. She was a survivor of frontier days before any sort of civilisation was in place – when a woman's life was always hard and frequently brutally short.

Jessica coloured. 'I don't understand your outburst. Explain, if you will!'

'I'll not keep house under a roof where the dead are disrespected and Christian ideals mocked.'

Mrs Dunbar's indignation found an echo in Jessica's own disquiet, but it was something the younger woman couldn't yet admit, even to herself.

'You over-reach yourself, Mrs Dunbar!' she said, her tone icy.

'That I do not,' the housekeeper maintained stoutly. 'The master's corpse is barely cold an' yuh let that fancy man in to live here, as if it ain't been enough him callin' at all hours with his damned inquiries about your well-bein'. It's unfittin', I reckon.'

'Mr Rymer is an – an old friend, and I'd ask you to mind your sanctimonious tongue, Mrs Dunbar!'

'I'll speak my mind clear, ma'am, like I've ever done, an' it'll please me for yuh not to have the honest hearin' of it no more. I declare me an' the good Mr Dunbar, who worked for your husband thirty-some years, are shiftin' out pronto. It's high time yuh learned how to behave like a respectable widder-woman – but then yuh're like to be no better at that than being a decent wife!'

Jessica looked as though she could throw herself at Mrs Dunbar and tear her eyes out. But Mrs Dunbar, though her senior in years, was still a formidable and heavily-muscled person, and she bottled up her rage.

'How dare you!' she stormed, hands clenched.

'I dare it for Boyd Blackwood's memory!' Mrs Dunbar said with the air of a woman who had more to say and wasn't in the least afraid to say it. 'He knew your stripe in the end, for a fact. An' I know the game yuh've played with his new will, an' others are goin' to, I figure. I told Miss Ellen, so yuh can watch out, Mrs High-an'-Mighty!'

Much of this was supposition and bluff on Martha Dunbar's part, but it gratified her to throw a scare into the worthless widow. It could all be wrong, but it sounded right the dark way she put it and the way Jessica reacted.

'Get out of my sight!' Jessica screeched. 'If you're not off the Double-B by nightfall, I'll have you thrown off!'

Mrs Dunbar scoffed. 'Plumb useless losin' your temper, lady. We're quittin', that's for sure. If yuh had a lick o' sense, it's that tinhorn yuh'd throw out. Yuh playin' with fire thar, "ol' friend" the moreso. Yuh'll git burned, an' badly!'

Having got in the last word, the miffed housekeeper stalked out, slamming the door behind her.

Orson Rymer choked when Jessica Blackwood told him about the bombshell delivered by Martha Dunbar. Not with wrath, not even on the cheroot he was smoking with a connoisseur's placid enjoyment, but on his mirth.

'The Dunbars! Damn it, Jessica my dear, there's no threat to us from those two drivelling old no-accounts. How much do they really know anyway?'

Jessica bit her lip. 'They witnessed the new will.'

Rymer was scathing. 'They put their marks on some bit of paper. They're too dumb to read or write.'

'But Boyd told them what it was. They'll gab.'

'A precious lot of notice anyone's gonna take of their bleatings. Folks know they're illiterate. They got hold of the wrong end of the stick, see? Let them gab all they like!'

Jessica's mind was not put at rest. 'The woman let slip she's spoken to Ellen, and *she'll* believe them.'

'Sure, and we know she's already approached Isaac Siebert who stalled her about any fresh will. He done that because he's another of the suckers susceptible to your luscious charms, my dear, and he's suppressed that goddamn will.' Rymer laughed. 'You got him twisted round your finger like a bit of cotton!'

Jessica shuddered. 'At a cost. I can't abide having his fumbling paws on me.'

'Aw, c'mon – a spunky gal like you knows how to handle the boys, and you've got to take the rough with the smooth. You've got shucked of a dotard of a husband, and look how you sorted out that fool sheriff. Don't deny it – you enjoyed that set-up. It was smack-dab made to order!'

'Ross Kemp was rude and horrible to me,' Jessica muttered.

'Well, he's paying the price in the state pen, I guess. His feud with the old man was right handy and he's got put out of our way into the bargain. He had the makings of an interfering bastard.'

'And so has Isaac Siebert. He might start making other – demands.'

Beneath the dark line of his moustache, Rymer's fleshy lips twisted. 'Yeah, Siebert is the real problem, not the Dunbars.' His black eyes glittered ruthlessly. 'And we can't have you being scared of him, can we?' he added with heavy sarcasm.

A fresh fear widened Jessica's amber eyes, and her lower lip trembled. 'What are you going to do?' she asked, a dread suspicion taking hold.

Rymer drew on his cheroot and studied the glowing ash. 'Not to put too fine point on it, my dear Jessica, I'm going to – secure your legacy and thataways my own financial prospects.'

His words were emphatic and quietly incisive, bringing a gasp from the beautiful widow.

'No!' she said. 'Not more killing, please!' She tried to keep the sob out of her voice and turned from him and faced the window, hoping he'd not notice the quickening of her breath and the heaving of her bosom.

'You betcha there's going to be killing,' he promised. 'I've already decided we can't be at the mercy of a two-bit, cowtown lawyer. He's shoved that second will in his safe, and he can get you disinherited any time he likes. We won't be sitting pretty till his mouth's shut and that damned paper's in ashes.'

Jessica swallowed hard. Ever since she'd lied about the notes that had fallen into her husband's hands, she'd known Orson Rymer was back of her husband's death. She'd tried desperately to ignore facts and persuade herself that the hypocritical Sheriff Kemp really had pursued and shot Boyd Blackwood down. She'd acted from defensiveness – unable to face that she'd been, even in the smallest degree, responsible for her uncongenial husband's death. But it was no good.

Rymer wasn't only a bloodsucking leech of a blackmailer who'd made her dance to his tune. He was a self-admitted murderer!

'Mrs Dunbar said I was playing with fire, letting you come here,' she blurted.

The gambler slid up behind her and placed his hands on her shoulders, his smooth fingertips intruding beneath the edges of her loose white collar.

'Now then!' he commanded. 'Enough of this tomfoolery, Jessica. Nothing so terrible has befallen you that you have to pity yourself.' He smirked. 'I'll look after your interests and you'll look after mine. A man's needs get awful neglected in a dump like Cedar City. It's time to loosen up a mite with your adviser and future partner.'

Jessica stiffened, doing her best to pay no mind to the hands now dipping shockingly inside her bodice. But it was a tactic clearly to no avail, and when she tried to shrug free, he ripped the light material open with a vicious tug.

She was exposed to his greedy gaze.

It was one thing to tease and provoke unlovely men made squirmingly impotent by the public eye that policed them on Main Street. It was another to choose to flirt with a dashing man who unconsciously awakened curiosity, not to say desire in the female mind.

But it was something different altogether to be subjected in the privacy of her home to an outrage.

'You beast!'

In answer to her affronted cry, Rymer chuckled lewdly. 'Now there's a sight the tongue-hanging riff-raff'd like to get an eyeful of!'

She clutched at the tatters of her bodice, weak from the unfamiliar sensation of degradation. This was a thing that didn't, in Jessica's experience, happen to women who were white, predominantly Anglo-Saxon Americans. And unlike when she was accosted by the stumbling drunks in Cedar City, there was no one to save her from Rymer's depravity.

She hadn't led a particularly sheltered life, but she'd never been forced into giving herself unwillingly, except perhaps inside marriage she'd chosen. In the cities and towns, in the gambling houses she'd once worked in, so-called 'easy virtue' and its questionable rewards had been the lot of those considered inferior by reason of race, creed or colour. The Indians, the Mexicans, the Chinese, the Blacks … only these, creatures of low morals assuredly, were obliged to release their pathetic bodies with neither the right of choice nor the benefit of matrimony to the pleasure of rampant menfolk.

Once, when she'd been living in Colorado, she'd been taken to the gold rush town of Leadville, where she was told that in 1880 there was a bordello for every 150 inhabitants. She'd found the painted, brightly dressed whores – and the atmosphere of cheap perfume and hopeless slavery that clung to their haunts – sickeningly repugnant.

These thoughts of her imminent debasement and its comparison to prostitution, paralysed Jessica, turning her knees to water.

Then Rymer pushed her savagely, so that she went sprawling onto a horsehair sofa.

'You'll not come the stiff and haughty madam with me, Jessica my precious! There's too much I know. And I mean to know *everything* about you before the hour's out!'

He lunged after her, trapping the supple, struggling richness of her once-proud body.

Orson Rymer, his lusts for the present sated, swung a blanket, a saddle and his own aching loins across the steeldust roan formerly ridden by Boyd Blackwood and went to seek out Jeremiah 'Snake' McClay.

He was in a generous mood and thought he might profitably put some pleasure similar to that he'd latterly enjoyed himself in the way of his runty dogsbody.

Snake was a totally unattractive individual in both appearance and character, and Rymer had been quick to note women found it hard to disguise their repulsion for him, which left him with a hell of a chip on his shoulder. Verily, Snake had something of a complex, and his evil, dirty mind was at its most inventive, his conversation at its most colourful, when he was describing what he might do to some saloon-girl or other, given the chance.

Rymer found his man alone, over the

spine of a hogsback several miles north of the ranch house, on the fringe of the brush and chaparral country. Snake was lazing in the grama grass, smoking; his mount was left to graze nearby with reins hanging down beside its drooping head.

'So this is how you drive the mavericks out of the brush,' Rymer greeted him.

McClay got to his feet, glowering. 'Since when've you bin the range boss, Rymer?'

'Just kidding, Snake. I'm no cattle baron. I live on my wits – and other people's lack of them. And I got easier chores in mind for you, too, friend. Reckon you'll like 'em a whole lot better than punching cows.'

He told McClay that trouble could be brewing in the shape of Blackwood's lawyer, his daughter and the Dunbars. 'Siebert I'll take care of personally. But it'd do no harm if a scare was thrown into those quitting hicks, and I'd pay you back one of them IOUs to know just how much Ellen Blackwood has figured out.'

Snake straightened his narrow shoulders

and gave his monkey grin. 'The ideas you put into my head!'

'Mebbe you could go calling on Miss Ellen one night soon as part of her dead pa's old crew… I'll leave the details to your judgement. Deal to her how you like, but there must be no slip-ups. When you've finished, you may have to kill her, of course. A great pity, her being such a comely gal. But I guess you'll see to it her charms aren't purely wasted.'

'I'll teach her a bit o' life first, sure thing,' McClay said.

Anticipation had already set the warped gunslick's mouth watering.

10

Death Canyon

Ross Kemp had an early premonition that the day was going to be like no other. For a start, his cell-mate Maloney got bawled out for talking out of turn in the penitentiary dining hall. There was nothing unusual in that, but for once Kemp figured the offending confab had been instigated not by the loose-tongued train robber, but by the other party – a new prisoner he'd not seen before.

'Button your lip, prisoner!' a guard snapped, 'Or yuh'll do forty days in solitary!'

The pow-wow was cut short but Maloney's spirit was far from squashed. In fact, he seemed cock-a-hoop as he wolfed the tasteless slops from his plate. 'Today's a loikly day, me kiddo!' he whispered with a confiding wink.

Kemp didn't know what to make of that, nor of the weather. Commonly, morning arrived with a swift drizzle of yellow light that presaged the sapping heat the convicts would labour in on the work gangs. But today, the sun didn't come up. During the night, a murk of dark cloud had stolen in. The sky was a uniform, solid grey. From such overcast, sooner or later, rain seemed probable.

The gloomy half-light was appropriate to Kemp's mood of depression. He'd thought much about escape; he'd also come to realize what his brain-racking produced was useless dreams, not plans.

The whole boiling of his thoughts was further agitated by a growing concern for Ellen Blackwood. Every time he came to thinking about the injustice he'd suffered himself, her beautiful face got in the way of the righteous anger that simmered inside him. The more he considered the surprising news about Boyd Blackwood's missing will, the more certain he became that Ellen was in peril.

If there had been a new will, as Martha Dunbar claimed, it was silver cartwheels to bone buttons that Ellen would be the main benefactor, since his widow had clearly fallen from the cattleman's favour. Mindful that a ruthless, back-shooting killer still roamed the Cedar City range, Kemp fretted constantly and futilely as he endured his unearned sentence.

He yearned to get his itching hands on Jessica Blackwood again – this time to shake out of her the truth he was convinced she could tell.

''Tis indeed a boon this cloud will be,' Maloney said with a mirthless grin. 'The poor-r-r light will be a-hidin' a multitude of sins, and our brows will be the less sweaty from our exertions. Begorra, a cool head can be a wonderful thing, you understand?'

Kemp thought he did, but only partly. It wasn't particularly like Maloney to be cryptic. He agreed, though, that obliteration of the blistering sun would be a huge relief. It made a hell-hole of the box canyon where they were forced to labour.

The prison was set in a bleak, treeless landscape. Outside its walls stretched a vast, rocky mesa. A short march to the west was a bowl, its shallow sides treacherous with loose shale and rocks. The bowl's rough centre was fractured by a deep rift – the sheer-sided box canyon where the state pen's inmates broke the rock and loaded it onto sturdy wagons, to be hauled out by teams of massive oxen.

The canyon was ideally suited for penal purposes.

A short way down from its one open end and entrance, a ledge jutted out from the side of the almost-vertical rock face. Here a guardhouse had been built. Its roof was the raw rock of the ledge, hammered back on the underside to some sort of level plane. Its front and side walls were heavy logs. Loopholes were let in between the logs and through these slits, those manning the stronghold could command a wide view of the entrance and its approaches and cover the area comprehensively with their guns.

Nobody could enter the canyon – or, more relevantly, leave – without being apprehended.

The whole structure was bullet-proof and amounted to a small fort. Inside, a big man with outstretched arms could touch the back wall of rock and the front wall of logs and his head might brush the roof. But it was a grand observation post, gave shade and shelter and was seemingly impregnable.

There was a blind spot, but if its constructors had realised it they had discounted it. They were correct, too, in assuming that while the post stood, it would unfailingly fulfil its purpose of putting an invisible seal on the canyon.

The convict party was marched in the gloom, chained together, to its workplace. The clouds hung low over the mesa as rolling, broken banks of mist. Without knowing why, Kemp thought an army could skulk up there and not be seen.

At the canyon, to allow them to swing their heavy sledges and not decimate their own ranks, the prisoners were released from the chains before starting their gruelling work.

But there was nowhere a man could run to before he would be cut down by carbines held on him and his fellows by the hard-bitten guards overseeing their strivings from on horseback.

'Git yore backs inta it, yuh straggedly-assed bastards!' cried the detail's leader.

No one argued with the order.

Kemp smashed rocks with a will, taking out his frustrations in the violence of the rugged exercise. When a wind whipped up and the first, big, fat drops of rain fell from the ever-darkening sky, he rejoiced.

'The stinking air could do with some cleansing, an' it'll settle the dust.' Kemp's choked words rumbled up from his deep chest to be drowned out by the splintering impact of the sledge.

More raindrops fell, less gently than the

first. Instead of being soaked up by the all-pervading, suffocating dust, they spattered it with deeper, sand-coloured splotches.

Soon, Kemp's thin convict overalls were clinging soggily with a chill wetness quite unlike the sweat damp that regularly plastered them to his muscular body.

The guards shrugged into the yellow slickers they carried lashed to their saddle cantles. The four of them conferred with one another.

'Much more o' this an' we'll be ketchin' pneumonia,' one grumbled. They had no reason to stay out in the wet when they could retreat inside their log-fronted stronghold. There, they could still keep their eyes and weapons trained on the prisoners and any possible line of escape.

'No lettin' up, yuh rats ... or yuh'll dance to some shootin' practice with yore heels fer targets!'

With these last admonitory words to their charges, they withdrew into the guardhouse.

The rain was ceasing to be pleasant, even

for the toiling convicts, glad of the change from sweltering heat. The ground around their feet became puddled and riven with rivulets. It was quickly churned by their efforts into a quagmire of cloying mud. This sucked at their sodden boots with the stickiness of glue and made the hafts of their heavy sledges slimy and hard to grip.

'Like ever, it's a lousy deal we get!' Kemp grunted, flicking the wet hair from his forehead.

But Maloney was fairly jigging with repressed excitement. "Tis a blessin', I tell you!'

'You don't mind this damned cloudburst?' Kemp stared in blank disbelief.

'I'm not mindin' at all, at all!'

Kemp spat out the gritty water that had gotten into his mouth. 'Then you must've turned plumb crazy,' he said disgustedly.

'You'll see, you'll see! To be sure you will!' the train robber lilted.

A mighty crash suddenly rent the turbid air.

‘Thunder!’ Kemp exclaimed, though there had been no hint of it approaching and it seemed an unsatisfactory explanation. ‘Close an’ all!’

Maloney laughed outright. Kemp couldn’t figure whether it was tears or rain that ran down his cheeks.

‘No, me boyo, no! ’Tis me brother Pat an’ his bunch a-comin’ to me rescue!’

A second explosive roar left Kemp’s ears ringing and, looking up to the canyon rim above the guardhouse, he saw chunks of mud and rock flung into the grey sky.

Then the rumbling began, and a fall of shale and boulders and stormwater began trickling over the top of the crumbling rim. For a moment it looked like some giant leak from a piece of broken spouting, splashing down out front of the guardhouse, pounding the terrace in one spot, raising clouds of misty spray.

But rapidly – in seconds – it developed into a torrent, and next a gigantic landslide.

Tons of rock debris and shale boiled over

the edge of the canyon down onto the guardhouse, burying it from sight. The surprise was so complete that not one occupant recognised quite what was happening; not one quit the place, though had he tried, it would have been a no less dangerous option than staying put.

For several minutes, the entire slope of broken terrain above the rim must have been on the move.

'God Almighty! What triggered that?' Kemp asked his cell-mate when the noise of it subsided.

''Tis Patrick Maloney, begorra! An' he's done us proud,' the outlaw bragged. 'There's none better at layin' a charge o' dynamite. That bowl o' shale mayn't be no railroad nor Wells Fargo bullion car, but when its results you're wantin', Pat's your man!'

From that, Kemp raked out the explanation of what he'd witnessed. The train-robbing gang of outlaws led by Seamus Maloney's brother had blasted an avalanche of rock onto the guardhouse to clear the way for freeing their convict compatriot.

The rain was still slashing down in sheets, but Kemp still had enough of his wits about him to figure that though the storm and its preceding, dusk-like gloom had masked the activities of the Maloney gang, it might not have deafened ears at the penitentiary to the dynamiting.

Also, so violent a downpour couldn't last.

'It's time we lit out while the going's good,' he advised.

Maloney didn't disagree. 'When they come out lookin' from the pen, sure 'tis they'll not be appreciatin' o' me brother's handiwork. An' wild stallions couldna be draggin' me back to the place!'

Four warders were already dead, or buried alive. 'Soon as the governor hears of this, all hell will bust loose, Maloney!'

Kemp was wrong. Hell wouldn't be held off that long.

They weren't the only pair with thoughts of flight. Fourteen other convicts, wild-eyed and wondering, saw that they were unguarded. One of them, a strong-armed, tow-headed fellow with a scarred face, got smart fastest. Of the guards' four horses, two tethered to a hitch rail had been caught in the landslide. The other pair, spooked by the thunderous din, had bolted up to the dead end of the canyon. Scarface set off toward them.

About half the convicts sloshed across the wet slurry after him.

The scared horses nickered and tried to elude the strange, violent hands that grabbed for their trailing reins. One put its right front hoof in a watery hole and its leg buckled. It tried to recover, but stumbled and went crashing to the uneven ground.

The shrill screams of a horse in pain filled the air, chilling Kemp's blood so that the rain trickling down his back seemed like icewater.

Instantly, the convicts were fighting amongst themselves for the one remaining chance of a mount. Fists flew and men picked up rocks and smashed them mercilessly into each other's faces.

These were the brutalised dregs of late nineteenth-century American society, devoid of all morals and compunctions. They fought to no code and gave a damn for no one, including their own honourless peers.

Badmen's agonised cries mingled with the stricken horse's screams and blood flowed freely.

Kemp was appalled, but Maloney gave no mind to the mêlée. He was heading the other way – for the draw that was the beginning of the box canyon.

The ex-sheriff saw why when four riders swept into view around the twisted upthrusts of slag and stone. A fifth horse followed at an obedient canter, responding to the tug of a long lead rein fastened to the saddle cantle of one of the riders. It was no pack animal but a saddled mount.

'Saint Patrick hisself, an' with a hoss for me! 'Tis time I bid you a fare-thee-well!' Maloney called back. 'Good luck!'

Some of the bloodied convicts who'd not

been killed or bashed unconscious in the fight for the surviving prison horse, gave Seamus Maloney pursuit, yelling to the arriving bandits to let them ride double.

The Maloney bunch, set for riding hot-foot from the scene, weren't having a bar of it.

'Outa th' road, yuh bums!'

Kemp's former cell-mate was putting his foot in the stirrup, when clutching hands grabbed him from behind.

The leading outlaw, a black-bearded giant Kemp assumed to be Pat Maloney, thrust his gloved hand through a slit in his slicker. It came out in less than an instant, wrapped around the grip of a Colt. He fired point-blank into the face of the man hindering his brother. A tongue of flame spat from the six-shooter's muzzle.

The bullet drilled straight through and redly, messily out the back of the convict's skull.

The shot was the signal for the rest of the mob to draw handguns, and three more of the convicts were cut down while Seamus Maloney swung aboard the led horse.

Unarmed, Kemp was in the thick of what was shaping up to be a wholesale massacre. All hope of escape was fast disappearing. He'd be lucky to come out of this with his life.

11

On the Dodge

Kemp was surrounded by ricocheting slugs. They smacked viciously against the canyon's rock walls and sang violently around his ears. All around him was the cussing of wounded men and the hoarse shouts of the unhit's anger.

The outlaws wheeled their dripping horses and prodded savagely with their spurred heels.

'Fan the breeze, me boys!' Pat Maloney ordered.

At this late stage, the scarfaced convict came lumbering up. He'd apparently failed to win the prison horse and was attracted by what his spiteful brain figured were the new pickings. But after being thwarted before, he'd paused to crudely arm himself, picking up some convict's discarded sledge.

He shoved Kemp roughly to the ground. 'Git lost, mister, afore yuh's topped!'

Scarface swung the heavy tool around his head like a hammer made for throwing. Kemp heard the iron head whipping through the soggy air above him and laid low.

With a grunt, Scarface let the sledge go hurtling towards its target. Pat Maloney!

The outlaw bunch's boss was hit in the back. It was a spine-breaking blow. He slipped from the saddle like a loosely filled sack of flour, bending in the middle.

'Dropped the bastard!' Scarface swore. And he rushed forward to claim his prize – the startled bay mare which was trailing its limp and dead rider from the stirrup where the reinforced instep of one boot was still trapped.

He never got to the horse.

With howls of rage, Maloney's three followers clawed still warm six-guns from their holsters and, turning back to the fray, emptied the remaining filled chambers into the convicts still on their feet. They were out for blood.

'Eat lead, yuh dirty swine!'

Scarface was the first to go. A third, red eye appeared at the bridge of his nose, stopping him dead in his hasty tracks.

Kemp, already sprawled in the dirt of the canyon bottom with yellow run-off swirling around him, froze. He didn't let a muscle twitch as the furious Maloney mob wreaked their vengeance on the convicts still running amuck. He knew nothing short of total annihilation would now satisfy them.

Weaponless, unable to intervene, Kemp didn't like what he had to do one damned bit. 'Oh, hell!' he murmured, playing dead.

The wailed pleas of innocence, for mercy, were ruthlessly ignored. Kemp's ears rang to the cruel cracks of gunfire and the splashy thuds of falling bodies. Even the convict who'd caught the prison horse wasn't spared. Both he and the hapless bronc were gunned down when they tried to charge by, out of the box canyon.

Finally, it was done. 'Dead, every lousy man jack of 'em,' a guttural voice said, thick with angry emotion. 'Let's ride!'

The retreating clatter of the horses' hoofs was swallowed up in the noise of the steady rain. Soaked to the skin, shivering with cold and horror, Kemp raised his head.

What he saw was like a battlefield. Corpses were everywhere. Not one prisoner had been omitted from the outlaws' killing frenzy.

A groan of black dismay escaped his lips.

Pat Maloney's bay mare had run off with the bunch but in the interests of speed, they'd left Maloney's body behind amongst the others, including the owlhoot's own first victim. 'What's a decent burial up against saving your own neck from the hangrope?' Kemp muttered acidly.

That reminded him he'd no time to waste himself if he was to avail himself of the opportunity so fantastically thrown at his feet.

'I'd be a locoed fool not to get going real quick,' he said, coming to his feet.

But he needed to do something unpleasant first, otherwise his efforts were doomed to be worse than useless.

Squelching over to Maloney's body, he unfastened the slicker and eased it off the still warm and flaccid corpse. Grimacing, he continued with the work till the man was naked. Then he stripped off his own striped prison garb and shrugged into the dead man's clothes. His skin crawled, but he knew it was something he had to do.

Kemp snorted. 'The britches ain't too bad a fit, but they stink high as a mountain cat's den.'

The last touch was to pull the convict uniform onto the dead outlaw. That mightn't pass muster for very long, but with any luck hours could be converted into at least the same number of extra miles before the law enforcers put out word that ex-Sheriff Ross Kemp of Cedar City was on the dodge.

He'd also be heading for the last place they'd expect – his old bailiwick itself.

His own ordeal and present discomfort

fled from consideration. Instead of rain easing to drizzle under a sombre sky, he saw sunlight dancing through the gold ringlets of Ellen Blackwood and the tender smile that reached right into her hazel eyes.

But he also saw a terrifying, unspelled danger looming over her.

He broke open Maloney's Colt and spun the cylinder, sending the spent shells from its chambers rattling to the rocks under his feet. Then he thumbed new bullets from the loops in the appropriated gunbelt and reloaded the Colt in all six chambers.

He felt better then than he had in an age. It was a long way to Cedar City. But he was one hell of a determined hombre and he felt pretty sure he could make it.

'Now then, which way's the railroad? Due east, I reckon. Without a horse I think I'll have to take the train...'

Working across country, alert every tense step of the way for the clangour of alarm from the state pen, Kemp struck his objective with unexpected ease. He near stumbled into a cut that carried the iron rails.

He scrambled down through thorny brush. It had stopped raining but the spiky twigs clawed wetly at his borrowed clothes. Then he made faster progress along the way itself, loping from tie to wooden tie.

The murky cloud was breaking up and the instant he came in first sight of an isolated whistle-stop and water tower, he left the track and detoured, so he approached the halt's buildings through cover, along the cottonwood-clustered banks of a creek which ran behind and below.

Stealthy as an Indian, he sneaked up. Two men were talking in the gap between a shed and a ramshackle section office.

One, an old-timer with a drooping dragoon moustache and in a badged peaked cap and braces, was conspicuously the railroad employee who manned the outpost. The other was a young cowpoke in faded range clothes, a saddle and bedroll at his feet.

Kemp figured him for a tumbleweed

who'd somehow lost his horse and bought a ticket to ride the train.

'Too bad, feller, that ticket's gonna be mine!' Kemp promised himself.

He moved in on the pair fast, Colt drawn and levelled, his thumb on the smooth hammer. He cocked the heavy gun the moment he opened his mouth. It made a threateningly loud click that underlined the grimness in his voice.

'Hold it, gents!'

A high sun was breaking through the clouds and his words cut like a whipcrack through the steam curling off the drying timbers of the unpainted buildings.

The old-timer gaped, but the young 'poke moved his right hand instinctively. It was hovering over the yellowed ivory butt of his kicker before he, too, froze into shocked immobility.

Kemp clamped his teeth on a sigh of relief.

'All right,' he gritted. 'Lift 'em, the both of you!'

'Lordsakes, mister!' the old-timer quavered, his raised arms shaking like he'd got palsy. 'What is this?'

'A feller in a little trouble is all,' Kemp said.

A distant hoot of a train's whistle reached his ears. He'd not been a moment too soon. In fact, he was going to need to move with the speed of a striking cobra!

He gestured with the gun. 'Inside, and quick about it!'

The cowboy shrugged and turned to go into the run-down office, but as the old railroad man followed suit and was momentarily between him and Kemp, the spunky sprout yanked down a lantern above the porch with his raised left hand. The heavy fitting ripped free, hook and all, from the rafter, showering splinters and spilled coal oil.

The old-timer went to his knees with a cry and the cowpoke swung the lantern at Kemp's head.

Kemp raised his gun-hand to protect

himself and caught the makeshift weapon with bruising force on his forearm. Glass smashed and tinkled, and more oil splashed. But some of it was thrown back into the cowpoke's eyes and that was Kemp's saving.

The youngster had grabbed out his gun. It boomed, and a wild, blind shot screamed over Kemp's head as he swung his bunched left fist. It contacted jarringly on the point of the 'poke's jaw. The stinging fog that obscured the young man's sight and had ruined his aim became suddenly absolute. His legs buckled.

'You chose to play it the hard way, son!' Kemp said as his assailant crashed to the porch boards. He turned to the trembling railroader, levelling his unfired gun again. 'Any more fancy stuff and I won't be so lenient,' he growled. 'Drag that feller inside!'

The old-timer scurried to obey. Kemp stooped to snatch up the lariat coiled round the cowpoke's saddlehorn and went after him.

A second, louder whistle warned him the oncoming train was still making progress.

He roped the pair of them together, working fast, trussing them up like chickens. 'Sure am mighty sorry about this, but I gotta do it. Now talk fast, old-timer – what happens when the train arrives?'

'She stops jest long enough to take on water an' any passengers. Drop the mail... She runs on a purty tight schedule...'

Kemp gagged the old man with a ripped signal flag and the young man with his own kerchief. That left him with seconds to fish the railroad ticket out of the cowpoke's vest pocket before the arriving train was pulling in.

'*Adios,* gents. And thanks for the help.'

The big brass engine bell clanged. Brakes groaned and locking loco wheels spun against the slick wet rails till the engineer kicked the sandbox lever, releasing grit onto the track in front of each drive wheel. With a loud hissing of steam, the iron beast shuddered to a halt alongside the water tower.

While the engineer and the fireman set to taking on water, the conductor leaned out from the rear car.

'Howdy, mister, yuh ketchin' the train?' he greeted Kemp.

'Sure thing,' Kemp said.

He hefted the cowpoke's saddle and bedroll onto his bent back. His face he kept as much shielded by his hat brim as he could, hoping he'd not be remembered too well later.

'Seems powerful quiet hereabouts,' the conductor observed, scanning the neglected, seemingly unoccupied buildings. 'Where's old Henry today?'

Kemp lurched up the steel steps into the car and shoved the cowpoke's ticket under the man's nose.

'Henry's got sick,' he mumbled. 'Gone down with the ager – the shakes, you know? The doc ordered him to bed for the day.'

The conductor shook his head. 'It's a scourge when the weather turns wet,' he said with conventional wisdom. 'Quinine's the best thing, mister. Stops them chills an' fever.'

'The damp rises from that creek down yonder something awful,' Kemp went on, turning and nodding out the door.

Kemp was acutely conscious that it was vital to keep the inquisitor occupied and on the train till it moved off. If he climbed down and took his curiosity over to old Henry's office, Kemp would be forced to run. On foot, he'd never get clear of the state pen and its environs before his escape was discovered.

The conductor rubbed his chin reflectively. 'Mebbe Henry'd better git the railroad company to fix a new timetable special for rain and the ager! When I was a boy, we had a reverend that got the shakes so reg'lar, he scheduled his preachin' to avoid 'em. His favourite text was "And the prayer of faith shall save the sick."'

Kemp made what he hoped would be taken for a murmur of interest. 'Is that so?'

'That's from the Good Book, mister.'

'Yeah? And would you know chapter and verse?'

'James, chapter five, verse fifteen,' the conductor shot back, proud to display his knowledge as well as his righteousness.

At last, the engineer pulled the whistle cord, the brakes were released and the train creaked and clanked into rumbling motion.

With relief, Kemp essayed a laugh of admiration at the conductor's last sally and lugged his borrowed saddle and bedroll down the long, nearly empty car to the farthest left-hand corner, where he sat on the last wooden seat with his back to the conductor.

'Cedar City, here I come!' he breathed.

He slumped down on the hard seat, letting his stetson fall concealingly over his eyes. It would suit him fine if the conductor and his fellow passengers were to think of him only in the part he'd taken on – an insignificant, drifting cowhand, down on his luck and without a horse.

But though he looked like a sleeping bum,

and the events of the past hours had been exhausting, there was no rest at all in his brain.

The second he closed his eyes, Ellen was there again, filling his mind's eye with her youthful beauty and intelligent composure.

And the possibility of some grave outcome to the news she'd brought him in the pen kept on worrying him half to death.

12

Snake McClay Gets Brutal

Snake McClay stood leaning on the porch rail outside the batwings of the Lucky Horseshoe. He'd barged out of the saloon after knocking back as many stiff drinks as it had taken to empty the loaned bits in his pockets. This served not to blunt his evil wits, but to bring it on home to him that he was hard done by in society. It turn, this strengthened his resolve that those held in higher esteem should be made to pay – and he, Jeremiah McClay, should receive that payment.

Orson Rymer had obligingly pointed him in a couple of directions that promised sport plus financial reward in the wiping of more of his substantial gambling debt.

Which should he go in first?

Ellen Blackwood was a dish that made him positively drool. She despised him, too, he knew, and that would add savour to accosting her. But he'd have to be careful. Her shop, the place where she now lived, was right here in the middle of town, and at this early hour of the evening the goody-goody folks were still up and about. Sound of a disturbance might bring them prying into what promised to be a spicy interlude.

A few female screams much later would be considered nobody's proper business.

So maybe it would be best to keep the best for last and turn his attention to the Dunbars. 'Snake, ol' son, yuh got strong will, that's what it is,' he congratulated himself, chuckling.

He straightened his narrow shoulders and swaggered off.

His steps took him to a meaner part of town, where the streets were twisted tracks with tough weeds and clumps of buffalo grass sprouting in deep ruts, and where the houses were no better than clapboard shacks.

Many of the poorly constructed dwellings were in disrepair and the district was characterized by a miasma of insanitary smells. It was a quarter where kids never got enough to eat and shivered in winter through lack of warm clothing.

It was also here, according to the saloon gossip he'd overheard, that the Dunbars had come after quitting the Double-B. They'd found a leaky roof at the vacant hovel owned by the woman's widowed Mexican son-in-law who'd gone south – across the Border, it was said – to visit family.

'Plenty o' housekeepin' fer the old baggage to do in this neck o' the woods,' Snake soliloquised dryly.

A small roofed porch was built across what McClay assumed was supposed to be the front of the Dunbars' retreat. He knew a thing or two about the art of intimidation. Electing to be perverse, he went to the other side of the shack, picking his way under a coppery-black sky past a clump of prickly-pear cactus and a heap of trash in some sort of midden. Disturbed bluebottle flies droned round his head, reminding him of the other touch he'd planned.

He stopped to tug out a crumpled mask from inside his shirt. It was what the westerner knew as a skep and was used by bee-hunters. It was a conical shape which fitted over the head to the shoulders and had slitted eyeholes. The mask was designed to protect the wearer when raiding nests for honey and the wax that was used widely in the manufacture of candles. But McClay's purposes had nothing to do with insect life.

He pulled the skep on and stepped up to a dusty window beside a back door.

A light shone dimly within. McClay rapped on the glass.

At first there was no response, so McClay tried again, applying his horny knuckles more loudly and insistently where a tentative 'Hello, the house!' might have been equally effective.

Martha Dunbar's voice called, 'Who's there?'

'Carlos sent me. Open up!' he ordered harshly. 'Or I'll smash this blasted window.'

Fumbling sounds and a thud indicted a bar was being removed, then the latch clicked and the door began to inch open, a woman's work-worn fingers clutching round its edge.

McClay shoved in his boot.

'What's this!' Mrs Dunbar said, stoutly unscared by the shadowy figure in the skep. 'Yuh ain't from Carlos. Yuh're up to no good in that stoopid mask.'

'That depends, ol' woman.'

'We're poor folks and got nothin' to steal. What the devil do yuh want?' The woman kept her bulky figure solidly behind the part-opened door.

'A li'le talk is all,' McClay said. Swift as any snake he was named after, the vindictive gunnie withdrew his foot and yanked the door suddenly shut, trapping and smashing Martha Dunbar's fingers.

She was not the screaming sort, but a howl of pain was wrenched from her throat.

McClay shouldered his way in, pushing the housekeeper before him and slamming the door behind him, setting the lantern flame flickering. He drew his gun and made a threatening gesture as though he meant to pistol-whip her, and she cowered.

Hank Dunbar limped forward arthritically. 'Yuh hittin' a woman, yuh bastard! Stop that!'

He flung himself on McClay's arm, digging his fingers in with a strength at odds with his deceptively feeble, crooked frame.

McClay bared his tobacco-stained teeth, turned on him and slashed at his head with the gun barrel.

'No!' Mrs Dunbar sobbed. 'He's an old man – let him alone!'

But her husband was incensed. Though his head hurt like blazes and blood spurted from a split between the wrinkles in his forehead, the plucky old fellow threw himself forward again. He'd successfully stopped the intruder from menacing his wife and this time his intention was different, and took

McClay by surprise.

Dunbar tore the skep from the gunslick's head.

'Trash from the Double-B!' he roared in astonishment. 'Whatdyuh want with us, McClay?'

'It might of bin friendly advice, yuh old fart! Like shut your traps an' go join that greaser son-in-law of your'n!' Then McClay hit Dunbar again.

Dunbar's bloodied head snapped back on his thin neck with a sickening crack and he collapsed in a loose heap of bones and over-sized clothes beside an iron-framed double-bed.

His wife wailed and, disregarding her broken and throbbing fingers, dropped to her knees beside him.

'Yuh've killed 'im!' she announced, her face ashen. 'Yuh wicked, ungodly wretch!'

'Hell!' McClay said disbelievingly. 'It was only a tap an' he asked fer it, the stubborn ol' cuss!'

'Yuh're finished, Jeremiah McClay. Yuh

allus were no good, I knew it, even if yuh fooled Mr Blackwood. "Snake" – huh!' she spat. 'They'll put a rope round your neck an' then we'll see yuh wriggle!'

McClay saw with startling clarity that he'd done murder. By itself that left him cold. But he'd done it in front of a witness, which stirred something akin to fear in his brain and brought him out in a sweat.

'Shut up, bitch!' he snarled.

Mrs Dunbar lurched to her feet. 'Yuh've got it comin'! I'm goin' to fetch Sheriff Tucker,' she said, made foolish by shock and grief.

McClay knew that even if he got himself a fast horse and rode like the devil out of the country, he'd be up against it from now on. He was out of money. There'd be a posse, telegraph messages, dodgers. Once the woman spoke out, he'd only be hurtling to the end of the road...

A tide of rising anger threw up the answer. It was obvious. The silly old harridan wouldn't take much killing. Just one bullet.

And a single shot in the night on this side of the tracks would bother no one.

Folks this dumb didn't deserve to live, come to think of it.

He swung up the Colt and squeezed the trigger.

The crash of the revolver in the confined dwelling was deafening. The heavy woman was flung back, a crimson splatter appearing on the grey homespun above her left breast. She clutched momentarily at the iron bed-end before she sagged and died without speaking another word.

Powdersmoke spread and made an acrid, reeking layer across the room.

The confidence seeped back into the runty gunman as fast and completely as the hearing came back to his ears.

No one came; no one called out. Before the outcry was raised, he'd be out of here and moving on to his next chore. There'd be no botching that one.

Ellen Blackwood was just a slip of a girl all alone, McClay reassured himself. And when he'd finished with her, she was going to die in any case. Orson Rymer expected it. Besides being a pleasure, it was going to be worth good money.

Yep, he'd do a good job.

McClay ducked out of the drab little house the same way he'd come, leaving it in silence broken only by the persistent *phut-phut* of a moth hitting the hot lantern glass.

A change in the chattering rhythm of the train's wheels had Ross Kemp tipping the stetson up off his eyes and taking a slanch-ways look out the window.

They were traversing a wooden trestle bridge. Far below was a foaming river, starkly white in the coming dusk. That gave Kemp his bearings and warned him it was time to think of quitting his stolen ride.

The train would soon be ending its trip, reaching the end of tracks at Cedar City, where it was likely he'd be recognised almost as soon as he disembarked. If he were fool enough to try it...

He stole a glance round the end of the seat, back down the car. The coast seemed clear. He stood up, but didn't reach for the borrowed bedroll or saddle. The train was starting to slow as the locomotive hauled the cars up the gradient away from the river. Smoke and steam blew past the window in coiling drifts.

Kemp walked down the swaying car, availing himself of the fewest and lightest of handholds, and only on the backs of seats that were unoccupied. He picked his way nimbly past carpet-bags and trunks to the very end.

He nodded to the conductor when he put his hand on the knob that opened the door to the small, open deck at the rear of the train.

'Get some air,' he drawled casually.

The conductor was engrossed in the study of a much-dog-eared Bible and scarcely looked up.

'Can't say's I blame yuh, mister,' he responded, but Kemp was relieved he went right on reading.

Kemp stepped onto the platform and gripped the rail with both hands, watching the wooden ties moving away from under the train ever more slowly as it panted up the gradient.

The country was familiar to him now, but he was looking at it from a perspective that was different. He had to be sure he made his leap at near enough the place he had in mind. His disappearance from the train would probably cause some action, maybe even a posse would come searching when things got added up. So he needed to be close to somewhere he could collect himself a reliable mount. Limp along afoot like some lame old wolf and he'd surely be trapped long before he could reach Miss Ellen.

He looked for a certain hilltop and eventually spotted it in a gravelly scar off to the right. Half a century earlier, a lightning strike had started a fire which had stripped it of trees and led to erosion which kept it free of vegetation, like a bald spot on top of a man's scalp.

Kemp vaulted over the rail, clung to the outer edge of the platform but momentarily, then flexed his knees and sprang.

He hit the sloping bank below the rail bed with his shoulder and rolled, crunching through scented clumps of sage and yucca spines, till he came to stop in a shadowy hollow at its base.

Above and beyond, the brass-trimmed, red-and-black loco steamed on, belching black smoke from its tall stack as it crawled noisily up the long gradient. When the train reached the top, and its rear end was a diminishing blob in the darkening distance, a shrill whistle came echoing back. Ahead of it lay only the down-run into Cedar City and it disappeared from view, swiftly gathering momentum.

Feeling safe from immediate detection, Kemp picked himself up and brushed himself down. Dusk was settling in and he set his sights on the distinctive bald-topped peak and made for it in as straight a line as he could.

There, in a remote setting backed by the forest, was a homestead – a log cabin, log barn and a peeled-log corral. Inside the corral would be mounts, because the homesteader was also a horse-trader.

Some said the man was eccentric, because he shunned the town and seldom visited it. Others claimed he was as mad as his unfortunate teenaged son, who'd been born an idiot. A few, including ex-Sheriff Ross Kemp, suspected he supplied fresh horses to fugitive outlaws, but they'd never had proof, and short of staking the isolated place out, they never would.

Fittingly, Kemp was going there tonight to do business with the contents of an outlaw's wallet.

13

Innocent Prey

Ellen Blackwood dipped steel-nibbed pen into inkwell and made another entry in her ledger in fine, copperplate handwriting. With a downpour turning Main Street into a muddy mill race in the morning, she'd given up hope of much custom and turned her attentions for the day to stocktaking and updating her accounts. Her millinery and haberdashery business, though modest in appearance, was popular with the ladies, both town and country and of all classes, and turnover continually exceeded expectations.

She was at a loss to explain the success, though the more acute citizens of Cedar City, including the former sheriff, could have told her it had much to do with her own pleasant personality and efficient manner.

Consequently, very late into the evening, she was still hard at it, recording, to her own downright surprise, the shop's astonishing disposal of straw sun bonnets and fancy silk bandanas, not to mention a whole two gross of spools of darning cotton in assorted colours.

With her single-roomed living quarters back of the shop also being her office, it was somehow not easy to break away from the work. Not that she had any overwhelming inclination to do so. Social life for Ellen was limited to visiting a few women friends and a weekly church choir practice.

She didn't have eyes for the men of the town, though every handsome young fellow for miles around had paid court to her at one time or another since she'd turned sixteen. The one man she'd admired had been Ross Kemp. But his life had seemed to revolve exclusively around the badge he'd worn so proudly. And now he was irrevocably lost to her in the state penitentiary, falsely accused and disgraced. She was adamant to herself on the injustice of his treatment, but frustratingly powerless to right it.

Linked as Mr Kemp's fate was to her father's cowardly murder, she also had strong suspicions that a conspiracy had been perpetrated involving her stepmother and the rich legacy of the Double-B property.

Like she'd told Mr Kemp, she'd pursued that line of enquiry with lawyer Isaac Siebert and been rebuffed. She remained sure, however, that the Dunbars had not been mistaken about witnessing a new will.

She was striving to return her troubled thoughts to her work when she heard the thump of footsteps on the boardwalk outside. Instinct as well as reason seemed to warn her this was not as it should be, especially when the late-night walker apparently shambled to a stop.

She turned up her lamp, her ears alert to every sound, a frown creasing the smooth brow beneath the fringe of golden ringlets.

A rattle came. Someone was trying the shop door.

Already in her nightgown, she pulled a wide shawl across her shoulders and wrapped it around her trim body. Bravely, she parted the drapes that cut off her private quarters from the shop and slipped through.

'Who's there?' she asked, loudly enough to be heard.

Through the window she could see the indistinct shape of the prowler on the porch.

A throat was cleared. 'From the Double-B, miss. Need to see yuh…'

Her immediate and automatic thought was that someone must be gravely ill, or worse.

'Is anything wrong? Is my stepmother–?'

'Yeah … Mrs Blackwood,' the rough voice answered.

It must be one of the ranch-hands, Ellen thought, though she couldn't recognise which. She quickly unlocked the door and swung it open.

She was instantly aware of two things, both distasteful to her. He'd been drinking –

his breath was laden with alcohol – and he was Jeremiah McClay, the one they called Snake and whom she found so ugly in looks and nature.

'Thanks, sister,' he said, sweeping past her into the little shop and kicking the door shut behind him. 'Nice li'le ee-stablishment yuh have here!'

'So it's you, McClay! What's wrong with Mrs Blackwood?'

'Why, I purely wouldn't know. Did any folk say there was?'

'You did! Or you agreed to it.' She felt suddenly very vulnerable. 'What do you really want?'

'All kinda things,' he said with a leer.

She thought from his manner and his liquored state that he was seeking money.

'I keep no coin or bills on the premises–'

'I don't want one measly greenback,' he hooted. 'You an' me's jest gonna straighten out where yuh bin spreadin' them lies told by the fool Dunbars. That an' have some fun…'

Ellen's hands clenched tightly on the hem of her shawl. 'Get out of here!' she cried fiercely. 'I've nothing to say to you!'

He reached out nonchalantly with a dirty-nailed hand and gripped her cruelly by the arm, preventing her from backing away.

'Let me go!' Ellen blurted, trying to shake off his hold. The shawl slipped, and with his free hand McClay whipped it away. Her skin crawled.

'Waal, there's a dainty sight!' he smirked. 'Fact, we won't bother 'bout no talkin' at all!' He jerked her to him, crushing her to his stringy frame in a powerful hug like a bear lean from winter's hunger.

She opened her mouth to cry out again, but he clamped his own over hers and she inhaled a sickening draught of whiskey fumes and fouler odours. She gagged, incapable of speech.

McClay laughed mockingly. 'Now c'mon! Yuh kin do better than that.'

Sobbing, fighting back a fearful hysteria, she slapped at his face. It was no puny blow, despite the delicacy of her smooth hand, and though it probably stang her palm more than his cheek, the courage of her resistance caught him by surprise. She jerked out of his loosened grip.

'Bitch! I'll tan your hide for that!'

With the lithe speed of a frightened pronghorn doe, she dived behind the drapes that curtained off her living space.

But the retreat was futile, deafeating her own best interest. McClay rent the drapes from their rod and plunged after her.

'A bed!' he said, the sarcastic, monkey grin returning. 'Mebbe yuh got the right idea after all, gal!'

Seeing nothing that could serve as a weapon to fend him off, she crouched in a corner, desperately curling herself into a defensive ball.

'It was you!' she flung at him. A bid to distract him with wild words brought the truth home to her with amazing clarity. 'I know it! *You were the one who killed my father!*'

In her extremity, she recalled his pride in

his marksmanship; his disturbing, debtor relationship with the mysterious Orson Rymer who'd now taken residence at the Double-B as a friend of Jessica; the mention of the Dunbars and what they'd told her. And she thought she saw the links.

The incredible logic of her deduction startled even herself.

'Smart – too smart!' McClay growled.

He was inflamed by the danger of the knowledge she'd revealed – and by the urgency of his repressed lusts. He seized her by an arm and a leg, and dragged and heaved her across the bed in the tangle of her disordered nightgown. His callous hands left angry red bruises on the soft whiteness of her skin.

'Oh…! You'll go to the gallows, you hateful, contemptible swine!' Ellen panted. But her face was white and her beautiful hazel eyes wide with terror.

'So what's a li'le more blood on my hands?' he scorned. 'I'll tell 'em in hell how I had an angel!'

He unbuckled his gunbelt and dropped it to the floor. The haste in which he prepared himself to grab the forced invitation of her sprawled limbs was feverish. And thoughtless.

She lay apparently in breathless defeat and compliance, but the instant his eager hands thrust forward to toss the skirt of her nightgown above her thighs, she rapidly came to screaming life, wriggled free of his clumsy grasp, and rolled to the floor.

Her slim fingers went straight to the butt of his discarded, holstered gun.

Simultaneously, a hammering came on the door of the shop. 'Miss Ellen! What's going on in there? Open up!'

McClay swung in confusion. Before he turned back to the girl, snarling in fury at his thwarting, she had the gun trained on him. With a disgusting oath, he promptly lunged to wrench the gun from her.

That was his second and biggest mistake.

What he achieved by this rash action was to trap her slender but strong finger between trigger guard and trigger. His own hand was closed on the barrel, trying to pull the gun away from her, when it went off with a flash and a roar.

McClay gave a great shout of pain and clapped his hands to his exposed belly where it was punctured by the unaimed shot.

'Yuh shot me, yuh vixen!' he groaned, and sank to his knees before keeling over onto his side.

'Open up! Open up!' bellowed the voice at the door. The man sounded beside himself with agitation, and the door shuddered and creaked as he flung his weight at it.

Incongruously at such a moment, Ellen could think only that this was a voice she'd not dared hope to hear in Cedar City ever again.

'Mr Kemp,' she said brokenly. 'Is … that … you?'

'It is, Miss Ellen! Are you all right? Quickly – let me in!'

Ellen dropped the still-smoking gun, snatched up her shawl and gathered it round the ruins of her ripped nightgown. She rushed to unlatch the door.

Kemp burst in. He had a six-shooter in his hand and his jaw was set to a grim hardness. But Ellen noticed most the gauntness of suffering imposed on his features and the tiredness in the faded blue of his eyes.

'What happened?' he snapped, sounding unknowingly terse and rude. 'A gun was fired. Are you hurt?'

'No, but Snake McClay is.' She gestured toward her inner, violated sanctuary. 'He broke in. It was him who shot my father, you see, and he – he–'

McClay moaned. He was still alive – just – but he knew he was done for. He struggled to lever himself up onto his knees. Blood was dribbling into the grossness of his naked groin and down his legs. It was a wonder he'd not already died.

'Kemp, yuh bastard!' he croaked. 'Thought I'd got yuh servin' time fer me in the pen ... but that high-an'-mighty bitch' – he nodded at Ellen with a twisted grimace – 'won't get the Double-B. My pard Rymer has got it all worked out a treat. Yuh'll l'arn!'

It was his parting shot – a vainglorious attempt to crow to the end. The guttering flame of pride drove him to resist the brand of inferiority that had marked him all his squalid life. Snake McClay was dying, but for sure he was still on the winning side...

Ellen shuddered at horror present and horror immediately past. She felt Kemp's strong, sheltering arm go round her shoulders and unabashedly turned and hid her face against his chest.

'What did he mean, and what will we learn?' she asked, anguish mingling with the relief of her escape.

'You've been cheated, Miss Ellen, and I was framed by the same people,' he explained as simply as he could. The ramifications of McClay's bald confession were starting to mesh with everything else they knew.

'After McClay bushwhacked your pa,' he went on slowly, 'he snuck up on me, brought a gun butt down on my head, fired my saddle-gun and lugged me off with my horse to where I was found by the Double-B crew. Then he rode up hisself, all innocence, and planted the idea in the waddies' brains that I'd killed their boss!'

'The judas! Why did he do this?'

Kemp gave this sombre thought. 'Because it was in his nature, I guess. His record bears it out.' He drew a deep, ragged breath. 'But like he said, the genius behind it is Orson Rymer's. McClay's unwise gambling had made him the tinhorn's pawn, though he'd buck at admitting it.'

Ellen was nobody's fool. 'And Rymer's game is control of the Double-B… Mr Kemp, I fear Jessica has fallen into this man's toils, and Lawyer Siebert has not told the truth either. How can I get to the bottom of it? The Double-B is more than my old home – it's my poor, foolish father's life work. It mustn't be bled to its ruin!'

'Amen to that. Though I've busted out of the pen, I'll never be a free man until we've gotten the truth out in the open.'

A new anxiety struck Ellen. God, what was she thinking of when Ross Kemp was a fugitive, putting his own life on the line? He was the man she loved and she was sure he had a genuine fondness for her, too. But circumstances seemed always incredibly doomed to keep them apart.

'Mr Kemp, I can ask you to do no more. I'm appalled and sorry about everything you've been through because of the Blackwoods. You should never have come back to Cedar City. You've helped save my life by doing so, and I'm almighty grateful, but now you must look to your own safety. Ride on! Leave the state – cross the Border before it's too late!'

It was a heartfelt speech, and better than pretty as colour touched her cheeks and her hazel eyes became lustrous pools filled with pleading.

But Kemp said gruffly, 'The hell with that! Get on some clothes, Miss Ellen. We're going to shake the truth out of your stepmother tonight.'

14

A Macabre Discovery

Kemp's intention, stated so vehemently that he'd forgotten himself and swore, carried Ellen with him. Her mind was in a turmoil. She was into riding garb and as far as the door before it struck her. This was the hot-headed impulse of a moment. At this late hour, the wide, double doors of the town's livery barn, where she stabled her pony, would be shut for the night.

She yielded to the dictates of common sense and spoke out.

'No matter,' Kemp said at her protest. He was steadfast, and his mind was astonishingly sharp and clear despite his long day's exertions and traumas. 'There'll be an unclaimed Double-B bronc still hitched outside the Lucky Horseshoe or some other saloon, I'll bet you. Snake McClay won't be riding it back.'

It was a clear night, the air crisp and clean after the day's rain. A full moon rode above, its light augmented by the bright points and spots of a thousand stars and planets. But the pair were blind to its beauty.

As Kemp predicted, they found a horse with the distinctive Double-B brand on its flank at the rail outside the Lucky Horseshoe. At fifteen hands, the six-year-old gelding was higher and heavier than the Indian-raised pony Ellen had recently been accustomed to riding. But brought up on the ranch, she was an able horsewoman, and Kemp adjusted the stirrups and cinched up the saddle confident she'd cope without bother.

There was no further parley. They slipped away quietly, out of town, and rode the twelve-mile trail for the Double-B spread at a fast lope.

The big ranch-house was impressive in the

moonglow. Its whitewashed, Spanish-style architecture was majestic in scale compared to the other buildings clustered around it, though these were no less mean of their type.

But within, the hacienda was in total darkness. Not a light showed at any of its open-shuttered windows.

Kemp glanced significantly at Ellen, who had made the same observation.

'Do we go on?'

She nodded. 'No sense in wasting the ride. And by morning the law will be on your heels, Mr Kemp. Let's speak to my father's widow.'

He leaned forward in the saddle to lift the iron latch of the yard gate and they walked their horses on in and swung down.

There were murmurings over in the direction of the bunkhouse, a corraled horse nickered a curious welcome to the newcomers and the windmill clanked slowly in the lightest of breezes. But the big rock-and-adobe ranch-house stayed silent.

They went up to the porticoed entrance and Kemp rapped his knuckles on a polished oak door with blacked iron fittings.

No one came.

Behind them, sensing tension in the air, their horses pawed the gravel of the yard restlessly. The scrape of their hoofs and the jangling of shaken stirrup assemblies and tossed harness rings merely underscored the silence of the house.

Kemp balled his fist and hammered the door. 'Hello there! Mrs Blackwood! Rymer!'

Ellen shrugged. 'The Dunbars have quit and there's probably no housekeeping staff. Orson Rymer goes to town in a buggy of nights – well some nights. But Jessica should be here…'

'That so? I reckon we'll be knocking till our knuckles are raw and calling till we're blue in the face,' Kemp said.

He put his hand exploratively to a shiny black knob. To his surprise, it turned and the door moved.

'Doesn't that beat all! The door's unlocked,

it seems. For Rymer, maybe. Why does he go to town?

'To show off his skills at the poker tables, I understand.'

Kemp frowned. 'Why in blazes hasn't Mrs Blackwood answered? There's something strange about this whole thing. Shall we go in?'

'It's that or go enquire at the bunkhouse, I guess.'

'No,' Kemp objected flatly. 'I'm a jailbird, remember? Let those cowpokes sight my face hereabouts and they'd likely get to shooting.'

Ellen shuddered. 'Another death is the last thing I want to see.' She added to herself, silently, *especially* yours.

He found a lucifer and scratched it into life.

'Figure it'll do less harm if 'n we just go in and take a look-see.'

Her hand touched his arm as they went forward. 'The parlour is on the left.'

In the seconds before the match sputtered

out, its flickering light showed Kemp the crouching shapes of comfortable armchairs and a sofa ranged round the room. An upright piano stood in one corner with a violin case and framed daguerreotypes atop it. His boot heels sank into the softness of carpet. Paintings were on the walls.

The spacious parlour was beyond comfortable. It was by prevailing standards opulent. But it also was clearly unoccupied.

Ellen moved past him and drew back the drapes at a window. The high-sailing moon cast in a beam of light, adequate to let them move around without stumbling into furniture. It also chiselled planes of harsh white across Kemp's grim, enquiring face.

'She's not here,' Ellen said quietly. 'Maybe she went out with Rymer. But there's the study and her bedroom, of course. Shall I give us some light?'

Kemp nodded, handing her another lucifer. 'The candle on the sideboard. We'll take it with us.'

Ellen went quickly through the house that

had been her childhood home with Kemp at her heels.

'Nobody! The place is empty,' he said with a kind of disgust when the search was done.

Ellen sighed. 'I've not seen Jessica in town with Rymer before.'

'Maybe there's someplace else she could be. One of the outbuildings…?'

'She would have returned by now, or called out when she heard someone come to the house, surely?' Ellen countered. 'I don't like the looks of this. Maybe she's had an – an accident.'

She had just put in words something like the thought that had flashed through Kemp's brain. But he said, 'Is there any other place she might go close by? Where she could have tripped or fallen?'

Ellen considered, fingers going to her lips in a gesture that Kemp found oddly stirring.

'Yes, there is…' she mused. 'It's on the Double-B home range about five minutes' walk from the house and Jessica wouldn't have gone there after dark. It's a secret glade

– well, that is father said it was to be used only by the family.'

'Does Jessica go there?'

'Of course. There's a lovely, tree-shaded creek and she and pa went there often in the hot time of summer to – to bathe, I expect,' she said, slightly flustered.

Once again, following impulse, Kemp said, 'Show me the way, please. She might have gone before dusk fell and slipped or something. While we're here we should check it out.'

Ellen agreed. 'If she's there, we should go and find her. It's been dark hours; she should have been back long since.'

It took them a spell to find the path. It was overgrown with tall, swaying grasses, and chaparral shrubs had sprouted abundantly since Ellen had last used it.

'It seems more accessible than this by day,' Ellen apologised.

Passage got no easier as they went down into the bottom; it was closely filled by a thickening tangle of cottonwoods, willows and mesquites. These trees shut out the moonlight and made every step treacherous.

Kemp heard the gurgle of a fast-flowing stream and when they glimpsed it, a silvery ribbon, he noted it was a good half-dozen yards wide. No doubt swelled by recent rain, it also looked at least several feet deep.

'Easy now, Miss Ellen,' he warned. 'If one of us tumbles down there, we'll be in a devil of a fix.'

Ellen shivered. 'I'm starting to get scared, Mr Kemp. I've never been down here in the dark … but it's not that. It's not a *childish* fear at all. I can't explain it quite, but chills are running down my spine.'

Kemp said nothing to that. Because he knew exactly how his companion felt. Inappropriately to time and place and purpose, he wondered if this sharing wasn't part of that greater harmony he'd always sensed in the girl's company – and had always found reason to deny.

Yet this was no place for warm feelings either.

A disturbed owl took off from above their heads with an angry flapping of wings. Far distance, a coyote howled dismally.

Edging cautiously into a patch of still-deeper blackness beneath some cotton-woods, Ellen said, 'We're nearly to the end of the path. There's a small dam of stones and a pool behind for bathing, and that's it. If Jessica was here, she–'

Ellen's words ended in a scream.

'What in God's name–?' Kemp cried.

The girl jerked back into him, turning and clinging to him in a way bordering on the unseemly.

Among a maelstrom of other thoughts, Kemp found this was something to which he had no objection. No objection at all.

'Something touched my face!' she blurted. 'There, under the tallest tree!'

'All right! All right!' he said. Unthinkingly, comfortingly, he stroked the soft, springy ringlets of her hair.

The warmth of him seeped into her, stilling her shivering. Gently, he disengaged himself.

'Don't look,' he warned. 'I'm going to strike a match.'

The lucifer rasped and flared into life. 'God almighty, it is,' he whispered in a stricken voice. 'It's Mrs Blackwood. Hanged.'

Jessica's body still swung slightly from where Ellen had blundered into it in the pitch darkness. She was suspended by a noosed lariat from the limb of the cottonwood that overhung the path. Beside the path was a large boulder from which she might have made a leap. The rope had bitten deep into the white flesh of her extended neck and her lips were purpled and thickened and the tongue an ugly protrusion. Eyes bulged sightlessly.

Jessica had never looked so totally unattractive.

Kemp dropped the match as the small flame reached his fingers.

'C-cut her down,' Ellen said, her voice unsteady.

Jessica was clearly past all help, but Kemp felt he should comply with the request, if only for decency's sake. By feel alone, he scrambled up onto the boulder.

From this higher angle and different direction, he could make out the macabrely dangling form in the cottonwood's denser shadows without the help of artificial illumination. But the only knife he had was Pat Maloney's penknife, which was part-blunted with rust, possibly from the rain but probably from neglect, too.

Kemp stretched out a long leg, to plant his foot in the fork of the cottonwood's trunk. He climbed out gingerly onto the tree limb. It creaked under his added weight, and he had to hack and saw at the tense rope for a full, stomach-churning minute before the last joined strands started to unravel due to the full, dead weight of the swinging corpse.

Kemp grasped the lower part of the rope and let the body sag down on to the ground below. It settled with a rustling of leaves and crushed stems.

Ellen was already on her knees beside the heaped form when Kemp jumped down to join her. Bravely, the girl fumbled to loosen the noose around the woman's neck. The terror of their discovery in check, she was filled with horror and despair at the wasting of a life in its prime.

'Quite dead and cold,' she said sadly.

Kemp lit another lucifer, the last. He almost wished he hadn't. His glance fell first upon Jessica's neck, the flesh pale and waxen, but with a livid, bluish weal where the rope had done its cruel work.

The second thing he noticed was a folded paper tucked into the top of her dress. This he retrieved.

It was a note of some sort, for certain, so he shoved it into his shirt pocket. 'We'll need light to read it, and nothing more can be done here in the darkness,' he said. 'Let's push on back to the house.'

In a sombre silence that was a communion in itself, they returned to the ranch-house. Ellen relit the candle in the parlour and Kemp unfolded the paper.

'It's Jessica's handwriting,' Ellen said

instantly. 'Did she take her own life?'

Kemp nodded. 'Yes, she did. I suppose it's what you would call a suicide note,' he said, swiftly scanning the scrawled last words of Jessica Blackwood.

'What does she say?' Ellen demanded bluntly, unable to contain her curiosity.

'She sees the sinful error of her ways … how such error led her from boredom and frustration into unwanted troubles. Finding a new understanding of right and wrong. Remorse … but despair at the fresh form of captivity into which she has delivered herself – dominated by a depraved Orson Rymer and having to accept the hateful attentions of Isaac Siebert to boot. How it ain't right, and she'd rather die than go on – uh – servicing such vile creatures–'

Kemp's grip tightened on the paper, crinkling it as he turned the sheet and read more. He took a deep breath.

'Here, Miss Ellen.' He thrust the paper toward her. 'Read it for yourself. There's no time for me to examine it thoroughly. It says

Rymer is planning more murder – tonight he's going to kill Siebert and destroy your father's true last will!'

15

Rymer's Final Hand

Isaac Siebert sipped at a nightcap liberally laced with foreign brandy and reflected self-approvingly on the satisfying quality of his life. For an attorney in a small cow-town he was doing fine.

He'd been through some uncomfortable moments of late, but now everything was settling down nicely and some of the compensations which had come his way had been mighty tasty. Jessica Blackwood had fallen into his hands like a ripe plum.

He leered to himself. No, 'fallen' was not the word. She'd been put there by none other than her late husband – that besotted old dotard Boyd Blackwood – when he'd handed over a new will for his lawyer's safekeeping on the very eve of his death.

It had been most informative, too, to learn of Blackwood's suspicion that his young wife was not averse to bestowing her favours outside the bounds of wedlock.

And how convenient when Sheriff Kemp had taken leave of his senses and shot Blackwood dead! He didn't know whether he believed Jessica's story that she'd not encouraged him, and it had been tricky going through Kemp's trial knowing the widow wasn't the rancher's true heir.

But now the disposal of the Double-B fortunes was virtually in his hands. Of course, the gambler fellow Orson Rymer would need a power of watching and the influence he exercised over Blackwood's widow was a mite regrettable. But never mind – the will that assigned the entire inheritance to the rancher's naïve daughter was the thing. With that in his possession, he held the whip-hand. It had been very smart of him to suppress it and approach the desirable young widow with his alternative proposition...

Siebert had put down his drink and was rising from his armchair to turn out the lamp and retire when he heard shuffling sounds in the next room, which was his office located on the lower floor of his house.

Judging from the noise, Siebert realised the nocturnal visitor was making no attempt to conceal his presence. More in anger than fear, he went to the room and pulled open the door.

'Good God! Orson Rymer … what's the meaning of this, sir? How did you get in?'

The gambler jumped up from behind the big desk. Several drawers hung open and the top was littered with papers.

'I opened the door and walked in,' Rymer said with nary a trace of guilt. 'Opening locked doors is one of my many special talents.'

'You've got a damned nerve, sir! Get out, or I've a good mind to call the law!'

Rymer smirked. 'I don't think you will, Siebert. Given our shared knowledge you might almost call us – ah – partners.'

With difficulty, Siebert swallowed his rage. 'You overstep, sir. I'm an attorney of reputation; you're a no-account, tinhorn bar lizard!'

'I wouldn't take that tone, Siebert. A word from me would kill the goose that lays your golden eggs.'

'*That's* a rich one! Spill the beans about Mrs Blackwood's possession of the Double-B and your own cosy billet in this country will likewise be cancelled. Moreover, I don't understand why Jessica dances to your tune, but if I tell her to stop it, she'll surely have to, or lose the Double-B.'

'Lordy, you're a puffed-up, ignorant bastard, Siebert. Jessica does what I tell her for the same reason she does for you. It ain't just you and that damned will that can dispossess her.'

Siebert bristled. 'What bluff is this?'

'I got *other* facts, mister, which can do that same thing anyways,' Rymer continued. 'So that makes the bit o' paper you're holding worthless to anyone but me. Point of fact, it'd be better if you gave it to me right now, seeing how's Jessica is getting kinda tired of submitting to your will – no pun intended, I guarantee.'

'Go to hell!' Siebert yelled, losing his temper. 'And get out of this office! The will is in my safe, and there it stays.'

He stood aside and opened the door, gesturing for Rymer to leave.

The smooth gambler shrugged and opened his hands and moved to do so. But as he came level with Siebert, he suddenly bunched a beringed fist and smashed it full-force from close range straight onto the point of Siebert's beard-tufted chin.

Siebert's teeth cracked together, his shocked eyes rolled and he slumped senseless to the carpet with a breathy groan.

'Arrogant idiot!' Rymer murmured, rubbing the back of his hand.

He shoved the door shut and tore at, and rummaged through the unconscious lawyer's pockets till he found what he was looking for – a set of keys on a ring. He crossed to the green-painted safe in the corner of the room and in moments had swung open its door.

Fingers adept at the swift manipulation of pasteboard flicked swiftly through stacks and ribbon-tied rolls of paper. Documents were heaped around his feet before he found what he was looking for.

Rymer nodded to himself. It was crude and amateurish from a legal point of view, and nowhere near as imposing as most of the papers he'd already discarded, but this was clearly the last will of Boyd Blackwood, rancher, witnessed by Hank and Martha Dunbar and bequeathing the entire Double-B holding to his dearest daughter, Ellen Blackwood.

Behind him, Siebert moaned, reminding Rymer his work was still far from done. Quickly he seized up bundles of the papers he'd tipped out of the safe and the desk drawers and heaped them around Siebert's prone form.

Then he pulled a flask from his hip pocket and unstoppered it, releasing to his nostrils the fumes of kerosene. He dribbled a liberal quantity of the fluid over Siebert's clothes, and even onto his hair and beard. The rest of the flask he splashed over the heaped papers.

Finally, he twisted Blackwood's last will into a long spill.

Ross Kemp borrowed the Double-B mount that had been ridden by Snake McClay and Ellen to hightail it back to Cedar City. It was fresher than the horse he'd previously ridden into town after buying it from the homesteader near Baldhead Peak. But even so, the twelve-mile journey took an hour.

When the lathered horse crossed the railroad tracks, heading at a tired lope for the part of town where Isaac Siebert had his home and office, Kemp, too, was in a sweat.

With the truth brought to light, he was determined to retrieve the will that would bring Ellen Blackwood her rightful legacy. To add to that, a life was at stake. It may be a miserable and undeserving one, but he'd need every witness and every scrap of evidence he could rustle up to clear his own good name.

Isaac Siebert's house was a large one, with a second floor. At the front was a garden enclosed by a neat picket fence; at the rear a yard and a small stable. Kemp noted lights in a couple of windows at the side of the house on the lower level.

Weary and saddle sore from riding again after being removed from horses in the pen, he climbed down with relief and led the blown horse into a patch of darker shadow behind the stable. Inside the outbuilding, another horse nickered.

Ignoring the stiffness in his limbs, Kemp vaulted the low fence and flitted round to the front porch.

From inside the house came a low mumble of voices. Angry voices?

Suddenly, a voice that could have been Siebert's yelled what might have been, 'Go to hell!' More words followed, but Kemp couldn't make out what was said. What he heard next was a crisp *smack!* like a fist striking another man's face.

'What the blazes!' Kemp muttered.

He tried the door and was only mildly surprised when it yielded to his touch. He ghosted in, drawing Maloney's Colt as he went.

But the house was silent now. Kemp began to wonder if he'd imagined the sound of a blow. Head to one side, he strained to hear evidence of further conversation. There was none, but the door to the parlour was open and a lamp still burned in the apparently empty room, while a crack of light showed beneath another door at one side of the passage. If he remembered aright, this was Siebert's consulting room, his office.

He moved up to the closed door stealthily, acutely conscious of the fall of his boots on the polished floor timbers. He put his ear to the wooden panel. What he heard was the rustling of papers.

Kemp debated with himself whether to barge in. After all, if he'd been mistaken about the voices and this was just Siebert putting in a late stint in his office, he'd do nothing except alert the lawyer to his presence in Cedar City. Then, unless he really wanted a life on his hands, the cry would go up and he'd be a hunted man.

But if, on the other hand, Jessica's scrawled and near-hysterical note was right, if Rymer was here and it was in fact him he heard moving about in the office…

He stepped back, frowning slightly, hefting the Colt. He wrinkled his nostrils. The puzzling smell that reached his nose was kerosene. Had someone knocked over a lamp?

Suddenly, his mind was made up. He unlatched the door, flung it open, and stormed in.

Lawyer Siebert was on the floor just about at his feet, groaning and twitching feebly, but to all purposes unconscious. Rymer was jumping back, dropping some crumpled document, his hand whipping inside his coat, no doubt to draw the hideout gun nestled in the shoulder holster favoured by his type.

'Don't try it, Rymer!' Kemp shouted. 'Reach, or I'll plug you!'

The gambler's black eyes slitted. 'Son of a bitch – Kemp! What the hell is this?'

'You've overplayed your hand, Rymer – that's what it is. Jessica is dead. McClay, too. You're on your own, and I'm going to see you hang.'

Rymer was recovering from his shock fast. 'I don't believe you, jailbird! You've broken out and you're on the dodge, that's what. Your lies don't scare me none...'

He'd back-stepped to Siebert's ransacked desk, and keeping his hand clear of his body he flipped open a cedarwood box and drew out a cigar which he stuck between his thin lips at a jaunty angle.

Kemp said, 'It's no lies, tinhorn. You were up to your damned eyes in a plot to keep Miss Ellen Blackwood from inheriting the Double-B like her father intended. You'd come here to find and destroy Blackwood's last will, and to silence this crooked specimen of an attorney. I don't doubt he'll be glad to give evidence against you to save his own lousy skin.'

Rymer sneered challengingly, but didn't speak. Instead he fished a match off Siebert's desk from alongside the cigars.

Almost too late, just as Rymer went to strike the lucifer, Kemp remembered the reek of kerosene that hung over the stunned man and the papers strewn about him – and he guessed Rymer's deadly game.

Kemp triggered, the Colt roared, and the match spun out of Rymer's shattered fingers unlit.

But the cornered skunk had sand, that Kemp had to admit. Even as a cry of agony was wrenched from his lips, his other hand went again for his hidden gun and he made a desperate dive to the littered, kerosene-splashed floor, firing a stumpy-barrelled .38 Colt Lightning the instant he drew it.

Kemp reflexively fired a second time, and thought the slug hit Rymer in the head.

Rymer's snap shot missed the ex-sheriff,

but its results were beyond wildest prediction. The flash of flame that spat from the .38's muzzle ignited the litter of kerosene-soaked paper in which he'd landed.

Tongues of fire licked rapidly across the papers and carpet toward the semi-conscious lawyer. Oily swirls of black smoke twisted above them.

Kemp holstered his gun and grabbed Siebert under his armpits and began dragging him out the room. The hungry flames plucked at the man's hair and clothes, till Kemp beat at them frantically with his bare hands.

He'd gotten Siebert out the office door, and out of immediate danger, when he recalled how Rymer had dropped a crumpled, twisted-up document when he'd burst in on him.

Disregarding his own safety, Kemp darted back into the room, convinced the paper Rymer had discarded was Blackwood's last will. It took him a spell to locate it among the other debris. But so far it had luckily escaped the full fury of the leaping, crackling flames, though its edges were starting to curl and singe.

Kemp shoved it inside his shirt. Smoke was now rising thickly, chokingly. He dropped to hands and knees and crawled under it, heading back to the door.

Siebert was still barely conscious in the passage when Kemp got back to him.

Meanwhile, inside the blazing office, Rymer had not moved. Kemp was sure he must have died instantly from his second bullet. He had no scruples when he slammed the door on the room in an effort to slow the spread of the fire.

The skunk's rotten carcass could be left to the flames; Siebert's place would be an antechamber to the inferno that surely awaited Rymer in the hereafter.

One month to the day later, Sheriff Alec Tucker rode out to the Double-B. He was met at the yard gate by Ellen Blackwood and his old boss and friend, Ross Kemp.

Tucker swung down from his horse thinking Miss Ellen looked especially pretty despite the grim experiences she'd been through so recently. She wore an off-the-shoulder dress of blue silk that offset her fair colouring and had on over it a dainty white lace apron. There was a becoming blush on her cheeks.

Kemp looked more relaxed than Tucker had ever known him, though traces of the rigours of prison life lingered in the deeper-etched lines of his face and the tinge of grey in the hair at his temples.

They went on into the house to enjoy a meal that was by way of a celebration of Miss Ellen's homecoming. It was also the occasion to tie up some loose ends.

'When Ellen's pa met Jessica, she was faro-dealing in a mining-town saloon in Telluride, Colorado,' Kemp told Tucker. 'He fell for her in a big way as we all know and brought her home to be his bride – to live a new life. What Jessica never told Blackwood was that her old life had included a tedious, spendthrift husband she'd deserted in Central City. When Rymer arrived here from Colorado, he recognised Jessica. He shot back to his old stamping grounds to check out civic records and confirm her second marriage was in fact bigamous. From then on, he had a hold over her. And after Blackwood was murdered, that hold tightened, because Jessica, of course, was never legally his widow or next-of-kin.'

Tucker shook his head, bemused by the deception and perfidy in others' lives.

'Waal, Ross, I guess it won't be long before yuh'll be standin' for office ag'in. Folks are right glad to l'arn the case ag'inst yuh was baseless.'

Kemp shook his head with a small smile. 'I'm going to have my hands full doing other things, Alec. I won't wear no sheriff's badge again. Ellen has accepted my proposal of marriage and I never did hold with married law officers.'

Later, after Tucker had mounted up and they'd waved him goodbye, Ellen asked, 'What's all this about having your hands full, Ross?'

'The Double-B is a big spread,' he said solemnly.

'Oh,' she said, temptingly. 'Are you sure that's all you had in mind?'

Then he laughed and took her in his arms and kissed her.

The publishers hope that this book has given you enjoyable reading. Large Print Books are especially designed to be as easy to see and hold as possible. If you wish a complete list of our books please ask at your local library or write directly to:

Dales Large Print Books
Magna House, Long Preston,
Skipton, North Yorkshire.
BD23 4ND

This Large Print Book, for people
who cannot read normal print,
is published under the auspices of
THE ULVERSCROFT FOUNDATION